Krista Kim-Bap

KRISTA KIM-BAP

ANGELA AHN

Second Story Press

Library and Archives Canada Cataloguing in Publication

Ahn, Angela, author
Krista kim-bap / by Angela Ahn.

Library and Archives Canada Cataloguing in Publication

Ahn, Angela, author
Krista Kim-Bap / Angela Ahn.

ISBN 978-1-77260-063-6 (softcover)
ISBN 978-1-77260-064-3 (e-book)

I. Title.

PS8601.H6K75 2018   jC813'.6   C2017-906503-3

Cover by Hyein Lee
Edited by Carolyn Jackson
Design by Melissa Kaita and Ellie Sipila

Printed and bound in Canada

*Second Story Press gratefully acknowledges the support of the
Ontario Arts Council and the Canada Council for the Arts for our
publishing program. We acknowledge the financial support of the
Government of Canada through the Canada Book Fund.*

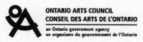

ONTARIO ARTS COUNCIL
CONSEIL DES ARTS DE L'ONTARIO
an Ontario government agency
un organisme du gouvernement de l'Ontario

Canada Council   Conseil des Arts
for the Arts   du Canada

Funded by the Government of Canada
Financé par le gouvernement du Canada | **Canadä**

Published by
SECOND STORY PRESS
20 Maud Street, Suite 401
Toronto, ON M5V 2M5
www.secondstorypress.ca

For my kids

CHAPTER 1

First of all, I know that if you haven't grown up eating it, *kimchi* can really smell funny. Sometimes when I go out of the house and then come back home, I can smell it in the air right away, even if we had it for dinner the night before. When you open a fridge with kimchi in it, the smell can sock you in the nose. But not in my house because my mom ties a plastic bag over the jar to seal in the smell. It totally works.

Grandma doesn't tie up her kimchi jars in plastic, and when you open the refrigerator door at her house, there is no mistaking that smell. I think her milk even tastes a little bit like kimchi. Still, even though it smells like somebody made a huge mistake, I kind of love kimchi. My mom says it's in the blood. If you can love a stinky food like kimchi it must be because you're Korean.

My sister Tori wouldn't be caught dead eating kimchi. She says she doesn't want her breath to stink. I think she actually likes it. I remember her eating it when she was younger, but lately she's become kind of funny about stuff like that. I've heard my mother grumbling about the "teenage years" when she's talking about Tori.

When we've had kimchi for dinner and Tori's friends are coming over, she runs around the house spraying air freshener. That's only after she tries to convince us not to eat any with our dinner in the first place and fails. Then she changes all her clothes and brushes her teeth ferociously as if her life depended on having fresh breath, which is always pretty strange considering that kimchi never even passed her lips— she was just *near* it.

Sometimes, my best friend Jason asks my mom for kimchi and rice when she asks us if we want anything to eat, and he's not even Korean! I've converted him over the years. When we were both in grade 3, my mom and I started by giving him tiny strips of kimchi, washing away all the spice. Eventually we moved up to unwashed big pieces. Now, a few years later, my mom says he eats kimchi like an honorary Korean boy.

Tori is very particular about not being very Korean in front of her friends. None of her friends are Korean. At her high school, there are only a few Korean kids and she makes a special effort not to be friendly to any of them, especially the exchange students who don't speak English and wear too much clothing, even if it's scorching hot outside. Most of them are new to Canada, but Tori and I were born in Vancouver, and for Tori that is difference enough.

Come to think of it, none of my friends are Korean either. I know some people who are half-this, half-that, and I always thought that it was a shame that no other Korean-Canadian kids lived nearby because it would be nice just to have a friend who you didn't have to train to eat the foods you like. But that's okay, I have Jason and he's willing to learn.

"There are leftovers," my mom told Jason as he rummaged through our fridge after school.

Jason looked at the glass container and removed the lid. "Yes! *Bulgogi!* May I?" he asked my mother.

My mom grinned. "Sure." She placed the leftovers in the microwave and Jason went to the cutlery tray to get a spoon and chopsticks. It cracks me up that he likes to use chopsticks. Even my dad asks for a fork at a Korean restaurant.

It was Wednesday. Wednesday was our free day. Jason and I had a standing date after school. We always came to my house. Jason had two brothers, one sister, and two dogs. It was a bit crazy at his place. His mom worked for an airline and had weird shifts. His dad was the manager at the local organic grocery store, so he was home more regularly than Jason's mom.

Jason and I learned what the word "ironic" meant in class last year and we both immediately thought of his family. We both think it's pretty *ironic* that his dad works in a grocery store because whenever we go to his house, there is never anything to eat! Since I'm not even twelve yet, I don't think it's appropriate to fend for myself at my best friend's house—that's what parents are for.

The last time we went over there after school, we were both starving. Jason's older brother was home, but he was not the kind of guy you asked for a snack. We looked in the refrigerator and all we could find were sauces, mustard, and mayonnaise. There was also some sour-smelling milk and moldy cheddar cheese. In the pantry, dried pasta and bran cereal. I think they order a lot of take-out for dinner. We figured the only thing to eat was the plain bran cereal and water. Jason kept apologizing. I mean it was okay, we didn't die of starvation, but I wouldn't willingly go back to his house for a bowl of bran cereal and water again.

On the other hand, my mom is always home after school and she always has something good to eat. She used to be a vice-principal of a high school before she had Tori and me, but she went on what she called "permanent maternity leave." That would be because of my dad. My dad is a very busy guy. He's a cardiac surgeon. He basically works at least eleven hours a day, then gets phone calls, text messages, or pages regularly throughout the remaining hours of the day. I know it drives my mother crazy. I'm used to it.

People always look so surprised when I tell them he's a surgeon—they open their eyes really big and say "Oh!" in a way that makes me think that they think it's pretty impressive or something. But I'm not that impressed. He's kind of a dork. He sings in an opera voice a lot. How can you take somebody seriously who does that? I sure hope he never does that in front of his patients. Normal people would never let him near their heart if they heard or saw him sing. Anyway, because my dad is almost never home, my mom always is.

While the leftovers were still heating up in the microwave, Tori came stomping into the kitchen wearing her earbuds and almost crashed into Jason.

"UGH! Why are you always here, Jason!?" Tori spat. "Why don't you and Krista get married already and start your lives together?" She grabbed a drink from the fridge.

There it was. The same old joke Jason and I had been hearing for years. We've been best friends since preschool. On the first day, I was sitting in a circle waiting for class to start—I don't remember this, but our parents tell us it happened this way—and Jason sat down next to me. He wouldn't sit anywhere else for the next two years. It had to be next to me. If I was sick or absent, Jason would refuse to go to school or stay there without me.

We've been tight like that ever since that first day. But we're older now, so if one of us is sick and going to be away from school, the other person will still go to school because we do know a lot of other people, but our first choice is to always hang out with each other.

To us, it doesn't matter that he is a boy with reddish-brown hair, glasses, and green eyes, and that I am the Korean girl at school who everybody assumed was Chinese—except Jason. He knew. We are friends. We have always been friends and we always will. We both knew it from the first day of preschool. Other people don't get it. We like to hang out with each other. We like each other's company. We make each other laugh. When we look at each other, I don't think we see anything weird or unusual about the fact that we are friends. Does it matter that my best friend isn't a girl? It does to certain people.

Jason always handled my sister with good humor. "Tori, I'm just sick of ham sandwiches. Korean food is such a treat!"

"Hmph!" Tori swiveled around on her heels theatrically and went around opening every window of the house. Then she stomped around spraying air freshener. I tried to ignore her, but she can be so dramatic sometimes.

Just then the microwave beeped. We forgot about Tori and sat down to enjoy our steaming plate of beefy goodness.

CHAPTER 2

After eating, Jason and I sat on the sofa to continue our card game. We had been playing the same game of war for three days, off and on, and nobody could seem to win. But then we heard a car pulling up in front of the house and Jason saw who it was—my grandmother. I could tell by the look in his eyes that we would not be continuing our game today. It wasn't that Jason didn't like Grandma, it was the other way around. Grandma often could be what you might call aloof, but to Jason, she was downright cold. I don't know why she was so mean to him. Asking her about it was out of the question.

Tori got along with my grandmother. They kind of had the same attitude about things. My grandmother always dressed very nicely. And her hair was always in a state of permanent curled perfection. It's like her hair didn't move. Even if she walked into the shower, I don't think it would get wet. Water would just hit the top of her head and slide right off. She always reapplied her lipstick after dinner and made sure her handbag matched her shoes. Have you ever seen old Korean ladies "out for a hike" in a forest on the North Shore wearing giant visors that covered their whole faces and completely inappropriate shoes? Like they might even be wearing heels? Well, that was my grandmother.

My mom saw that Jason was reaching for his backpack and said, "Why are you going home already?"

Then came the knock on the door and my mom looked out and saw the car. She gave him a knowing look and said, "Oh, okay."

When Grandma came over, she always brought her special soup. It was *tteokguk*, a beef broth with sliced rice cake rounds that get a bit soft in the soup

It was Jason's food kryptonite. He just couldn't handle it. We eat it almost every time Grandma comes over, and it's pretty tasty to me, but it is the one dish that makes Jason gag. The first and only time he tried it, he didn't chew the rice cake properly, and it slid down his throat and then got stuck. He turned a deep shade of purple and almost died. My mom freaked out and slapped him on the back and yelled "Spit it out! Spit it out!" He ended up finally swallowing the rice cake, but he never could, or would, try it again.

He would not be staying for dinner today. Plus, he had very quietly whispered to me once that he thought my grandmother was kind of scary. I can't blame him. She kind of is. Especially when she's gesturing and talking in Korean to Jason, even though she knows he doesn't understand. I can see how it makes Jason uncomfortable. The worst part is, she could actually speak English to Jason—if she wanted to, but she doesn't.

Jason tied up his shoes just as Grandma entered the house. She just stared at him, and he said, "Hello, Mrs. Kim." She gave him the slightest of head nods, like I mean barely a muscle moved in her neck.

ANGELA AHN

"Bye Krista, bye Mrs. Kim." He waved at my mom. "Thank you for the leftover bulgogi. It was delicious!"

Grandma raised her eyebrows when Jason said bulgogi. After the door closed, she said to my mom, "Why that boy always here?"

My mom said, "He's Krista's best friend."

"Krista!" Grandma turned and barked at me. "Soup in car." Did I mention that my grandmother doesn't like me either? I sighed, but I tried not to sigh loud enough for her to hear, and said, "Okay, Grandma, I'll go get it."

She prepared the pot of soup at home and then transferred it to our house in a cardboard banana box that she got from the grocery store. That way, the pot was secure in the trunk and couldn't slide around. The banana box usually had other Korean food in it too. Grandma loved to feed my dad. Since my dad was a surgeon, she pretty much thought he was the perfect son. Grandpa died a few years ago, so she was on her own. She came over at least once a week now, and she always brought food to our house just so she could watch Dad eat it. A little bit creepy, I thought.

When I entered the house, I could hear Grandma saying, "Alice, she never get married if she dress like that! Tomboy! Krista, she must stop playing with boys and acting like boy. Disgraceful. Look at her shoes. So terrible!" She was talking about my running shoes. They were getting a little shabby, but I didn't think they were totally ready for the garbage yet. Her comment pretty much summed up what my grandmother thought about me—awkward tomboy who was never going to get a good husband. Grandma thinks every girl's goal in life should be to marry a doctor, or to have a son who becomes a doctor.

I slammed the door closed so they could hear me and stop talking about me. I looked at what I was wearing. Jeans, a little roughed-up around the knees, but no actual holes yet, white ankle socks, and a black t-shirt. I know I don't dress "fancy" like some girls, but I like to be comfortable. My grandmother just doesn't like the fact that I don't care about how I look the way she does.

Tori came downstairs just then. Grandma smiled. "Tori, *aigoo* so beautiful!" She gushed about Tori's looks all the time. Tori was the grandchild she adored. We all know she is the pretty one, and I am the "other one." Tori dressed very fashionably and always seemed to look put together. She took time in the morning to get dressed and even wore a little makeup now that she was in high school.

My mom leaned over to me and whispered, "You're beautiful too, Krista. Don't forget that."

Whatever, Mom. I rolled my eyes. My mom always tried to make me feel equal to Tori, but I wasn't blind. My grades weren't even as good as Tori's.

Grandma started getting dinner ready for us. We have a don't-wait-for-Dad policy in our house. If he's not home by 6pm, too bad, we're eating. Today, we ate without him.

When he finally came home, he dropped his cell phone, pager, and car keys on the hall table and said, "How was your day, kiddo?" He gave everybody their usual kiss and for me, a hair rumple. He wouldn't dare touch Tori's hair anymore.

"Good. Why are you so late?" I asked him.

"Sorry, emergency at the hospital," he replied.

He was still wearing his hospital scrubs, which was usually okay, but sometimes he came home with dried blood on him without even realizing it—like today.

"Did anybody die?" I asked, pointing to the blood on his top. I always wanted to know if somebody died.

"Gross, Krista. Why do you care so much about people having heart attacks and dying?" Tori said as she sat on the sofa reading a fashion magazine.

"I just want to know!"

"Krista, nobody died today." My dad grinned. "Does that disappoint you?"

"Well, a little bit," I answered truthfully.

"Girls, let your dad eat," my mom interjected. "Grandma has been waiting for him for hours."

My grandmother busied herself warming up the soup for my dad and uncovered all the little plates of *banchan* she had kept under plastic wrap while we waited for him. She seemed really happy. Like, truly happy serving my dad dinner. My mom never looked that happy serving us dinner. She usually seemed agitated and busy trying to get it all ready, but Grandma floated around the kitchen. She was even wearing pearls today. She likes to look good even while standing over a hot stove. I just do not understand that woman sometimes.

CHAPTER 3

This year, my teacher's name is Mrs. June. She has
some crazy long last name, so she told us we could
just call her Mrs. June to make it easy for everybody.
So far, class was okay. Jason and I worry at the end
of every year that they will put us in different classes.
My mom and Jason's mom always have meetings
with the principal to make sure they don't split us
up. I heard them talking about it once. They think
it's important for us to stay in the same class. It's a
pretty big school and there is always more than one
class for each grade. So this year, when we got our

class assignments, we let out our usual sighs of relief. We don't have to sit together all the time, we're not that dependent on each other, but we just couldn't imagine what to do with ourselves if we weren't in the same class.

Mrs. June likes to start each morning by having us do yoga. She says it's calming and helps us focus. I try to take it seriously, but it's hard. I don't like sticking my butt in the air and looking between my legs at my classmates. I try to keep my eyes closed so I don't giggle. But most of the time, somebody loses it.

"That's enough, Marcus!" Mrs. June warned. Marcus was the worst. He didn't take anything seriously. He always set off other kids in the class. I tried to never be around Marcus during yoga time. "Breathe in and out. Slowly, take a full, deep, cleansing breath." Mrs. June really believed in this stuff. I kind of liked the feeling of the blood rushing into my head and how I felt when I finally stood upright again. It did clear my mind. I wouldn't have admitted that though, because we were all supposed to be of the opinion that this morning yoga was stupid.

After some more stretching, Mrs. June asked us to settle into our desks and said, "Because next month is Heritage Month, we will be starting a new unit on family today. We're going to be spending a lot of time on this unit over the next few weeks, so I hope that you are ready to talk to your family and learn about the country or countries or part of the world where you and your family are from. We are going to the library to start some preliminary research. I'm not asking you to do a family tree, I'm just asking that you explore your background in some way. Canada is mostly made up of immigrants, after all. My parents came from Hungary, and that's where I was born. I want you to learn about where you come from." She started passing out sheets of paper with information about our projects.

I groaned. Oh great, I get to be the Korean ambassador to my school. People will ask me stuff like, "How do you say *fart* in Korean?" and think it's *hilarious*. Well, actually I do know how to say it in Korean, *bangu*, but don't be fooled into thinking that I know any more than that. We just don't speak Korean in my house. My parents speak English to each other. Grandma speaks Korean to my dad, but I honestly don't think he understands much of what she's saying because she just ends up switching to English anyway. The only time my mom speaks Korean is when she's saying the names of Korean dishes in a restaurant. My dad on the other hand, doesn't even try to say the names in Korean. He just points to pictures or says the number next to the dish on the menu.

"Mrs. June!" shouted Emma. "This is not fair. I am quarter Chinese, quarter Malaysian, quarter German, and quarter Czech. I have to do way more work than somebody like…Krista!"

I mean really, is it my fault that both my parents are Korean? Geez, Emma needs to relax. She is one of those girls I never spend any time with and I really don't care what she thinks anyway, but why point *me* out?

"Yeah!" seconded Evan. "My parents told me once that I was like the human version of a mutt. I'm from so many different countries! Do I have to research *all* of them?"

Mrs. June stopped moving and looked very serious. She remained dead calm in the face of all this rebellion. She said, "Class. You are the sum of all your parts. You must know what it means to be all those parts of you. If you need to explore eight or twelve countries, ethnic groups, or religions, it doesn't matter. Which one would you leave out? Which part of you will you be too lazy to discover? That grandmother whose eyes you have? Will you forget her? Or that great-grandfather who nearly died traveling to this country whose last name you still carry? Will you say, 'No, he's too much work'?"

We all got very quiet. Nobody was complaining anymore. There was lots of paper shuffling, downcast eyes, and shoes scraping the floor. "What makes you *you*? That is the point of this project. You will see from the description that it is quite open-ended. I do not want a list of facts and figures about a country. Too easy, too boring. I want you to tell me how this country or countries have impacted you and your life. Start with big ideas and then, if you want to, go small. This may be quite challenging for some of you, but I am confident that if you talk to your parents or grandparents or cousins or aunts or uncles, you will find something that you can use to tell an interesting and unique story."

Jason looked at me from across the room with his scared face. Mrs. June had only been our teacher for a couple of weeks, and so far she had been pretty easy going. But today she was presenting us with a pretty difficult project and we had upset her. I knew exactly how Jason felt. Even though I want my independence for most things, I'm still a kid, and I like to be told what to do for school projects.

Nobody said anything negative for the rest of the morning as we settled down to tables in the library and Mrs. Germaine, the librarian, gave us the "talk"—the talk you get every time you do a research project—about plagiarism and copying and using your own words. We all listened politely. I don't think anybody was stupid enough to say anything sassy right now, what with the mood Mrs. June was in.

When the bell rang for recess, we ran back to our class, grabbed our jackets, and headed outside to brave the downpour. Our school has a rain-or-shine policy—we are never allowed to stay inside during recess and lunch. They want us to get outside and get some exercise and fresh air, never mind all the rain. Sometimes I hate Vancouver.

As I opened the door and received a blast of cool air and drizzle on my face, Jason put up his hood and said, "So, I'm thinking tartans!"

"Being Scottish is so easy," I grumbled as I zipped up. "What, are you just going to print some plaid pictures off the Internet?"

"She said it was open-ended!"

"I think she wants a bit more effort than that, Jason."

"Do you have any idea of what you want to do?" he asked.

"I guess I'm the official representative of Korea," I said as I shrugged.

"No, like what specifically?"

"I specifically have no clue," I replied.

"Well, when Mrs. June was talking, I couldn't help but think of your grandma and how she likes to bring your dad food every week."

"Go on." I stopped and stared at him.

"I dunno, I just thought you could do something about Korean food."

Huh. Maybe he was on to something. I started thinking about food, possibly because I was so hungry, and I was lost in thought when Madison Wong stopped me.

"Hey, Krista!" she said. Madison and I were friendly, but not friends. She and Emma hung out a lot.

"Hi, Madison," I scrunched up my nose and looked at her through the rain. I wiped some rain off my nose.

"I sent you an email this morning, check it later okay?" She gave Jason a funny look that I couldn't figure out.

"Okay," I replied, slightly confused. She had never sent me an email before. I guess if you had to describe Madison, you'd say she was one of the popular girls. She was always very well dressed, but it always seemed to me that she was slightly *overdressed*. Madison wears a lot of sparkly shoes. She always has. She has a sparkly shoe addiction. I clearly remember she wore ballet flats to Sports Day last year. She kind of reminded me of my grandmother for some reason. Also, she never wears a raincoat. She wears denim jackets and bomber jackets and other materials that seem to soak up, not repel water.

But aside from what I thought was impractical dressing for school, she just seemed more mature than all the other girls. She seemed to draw people to her. She wasn't ever silly or funny or loud. She was kind of a natural leader.

When she walked away with her squad of friends, Jason said, "You want to check right now?" Jason pulled out his cell phone, which he wasn't supposed to have at school.

"Jason!" I whispered. "Put it away!"

"Nobody's looking, Krista. Here, log in." He passed it to me.

I hated the idea of getting caught, but I really wanted to know what Madison's email was all about.

I stared at the email, a little bit stunned.

"It's an invitation to her birthday party," I finally managed to say.

"Oh, okay," Jason said.

"Jason. You'll never believe it, but it's a theme party. The theme is Red Carpet Party."

"You mean like an awards show 'Red Carpet'?" Jason used his fingers to do air quotations.

I sighed and looked up at the sky. If there was one thing I hated, it was wearing a dress.

It was a lot to think about. At home after school, I plunked myself down on my bed to think. A big school project, for which I had no real ideas, and Madison's invitation. I was the only one who hadn't replied by the end of the day. On the list was her usual group of friends, but she also included a few surprise guests, me being one of them. I couldn't figure out why.

"I hear you've been invited to a party," Tori said, barging into my room without knocking. I hate when she does that.

"How do you know?" I asked, surprised.

"A bunch of your loser classmates have older sisters who go to my school you know." She sat down on my bed. "So, what are you going to wear? I assume you'll need my help."

"I haven't even decided to go yet," I told her. Why was she being so nice to me, anyway?

"What? It could be really cool. You should think about it."

"You know I don't like dressing up. So what you think might be cool might actually be awkward and humiliating for me. Ever think about that? And also, I'm a bit busy being Korea's lone representative at the school. It's been a crazy day!" I was getting pretty worked up.

"What, a Cultural Fair or something?"

"No, Heritage Month."

"Oh Mrs. June's project! I totally remember that." She half-laughed. "I asked Grandma if I could borrow her Korean dress. It was very uncomfortable and I felt like a total loser because it is so big and not flattering."

"You wore it to school?" I asked.

"Yes, it was part of my project. I did a whole thing about traditional Korean clothes." Leave it to my fashion-obsessed sister to work clothes into a school project.

She stood up suddenly and clapped her hands together. "I still have it, you know, the Korean dress."

"I believe it's called a *hanbok*," I said smugly.

She kind of scrunched her face at me and gave me a sneer. She hates it when I correct her. I rarely get a chance, so when an opportunity comes my way I grab it.

"Krista, I have a great idea!" Tori was sounding a little too excited. She jumped up and ran out of my room, leaving me very confused and alone.

CHAPTER 4

We went to the library to research our projects again the next day. I was a little bit stumped. After Tori and I had talked, she hadn't really helped me figure out what I was going to do. She had just disappeared into her room. So while we were in the library, I grabbed an old encyclopedia off the shelf because I actually like flipping pages instead of staring at a screen. I guess I'm old-fashioned, but I still like books.

I looked up Korea. I started skimming the page by glancing at the subheadings: Three Kingdoms, Mongol Empire, Hermit Kingdom, Annexation by

Japan, Soviet Influence, War. That's pretty depressing. I kept flipping. None of that stuff interested me. Then I saw the entry about cuisine. This was something I understood. I thought about what Jason had said to me earlier too, about my grandmother and the way she was so happy feeding her son Korean food. I remembered how my mom always said that certain foods were "in the blood." I had found my topic.

I realized I couldn't ask my mom for any help—the kimchi at our house came from Grandma. My mom had never made it before, and she bought most of the banchan in our fridge from the Korean market downtown. Her Korean food was not authentic enough. I hated the idea of it, but I knew who I needed to ask.

I slammed the encyclopedia shut and sunk back into my seat. I let out a huge sigh. Jason looked over at me. "You okay?" he asked.

"No, I'm not," I replied.

"What's up?" He put his pencil down and looked at me.

"I think I need to ask Grandma for help," I sighed.

"Oh geez, I'm sorry about that," he said. "Why?"

"Because my mom buys her Korean food pre-marinated and pre-made from the Korean store," I said.

"Huh?" he replied.

"Oh sorry, I forgot you weren't reading my mind," I continued. "I think you were onto something when you suggested I do something food-related for my project."

"I am quite smart." He smiled.

"Yes, you are the smartest boy I know, and the funniest."

"Don't forget handsome!"

"Okay, okay, we took that too far. Anyway, I need to ask Grandma for help and it might kill me to ask her for it," I said.

Mrs. June walked by and said, "Everything okay here, Krista? Jason?"

I hated sneak attacks by teachers. "Uh, yes! Great! Fine!" I stammered.

She didn't look like she believed me, but she did me a favor and walked away anyway.

"Who knows," Jason said, "your grandmother might surprise you." How could he always manage to be so optimistic and positive?

After school, I knew what I had to do, but it took me forever. I stared at the phone for a long time before I got the courage to call Grandma. I was pretty nervous. I don't remember ever calling her up and asking for her help. The phone rang three times, and I almost hung up. She picked up on the fourth ring. "*Yoboseyo?*" she said. She has lived in Canada for decades, but she still doesn't answer the phone in English.

"Hi, Grandma, it's Krista," I said.

"Krista. Something wrong with your dad? Why you calling?" Grandma sounded worried.

"No, Grandma, he's fine. We're all fine. I just have something to ask you," I started carefully.

I paused. There was dead air. She was waiting for me to continue.

"Um, so…we're doing this project at school," I said. Still nothing. I could just hear her breathing. I took a deep breath and continued. "We're supposed to be exploring our background, for Heritage Month." I stopped, waiting to hear something on the other end. Nothing. I kept going. "But it's not like a normal project. I'm supposed to find out something about Korea or being Korean that is different."

"What you mean?" she finally said.

"That's just it. I can kind of choose what I want to do," I said. I paused for a little bit before I said, "I want to do Korean food."

"What 'do Korean food?' Eh?" My grandmother sounded confused.

"I want to learn about Korean food, Grandma. I want to find out what it is that makes me Korean, and I think it's the food." I was starting to ramble now. "You know how I love kimchi and rice and soup and bulgogi and I always have. I just ate it. I always just eat it. But with Jason for example, he thought kimchi was weird at first and it's only because he's my friend that he likes it now, because he's not Korean. He wasn't born knowing it or liking it. But I was. Do you understand what I am talking about?"

"Jason like kimchi?" Grandma sounded surprised.

"Yes, Grandma, he does."

"So you want to learn something?" she asked.

"Yes, yes, I do. Will you teach me some stuff? You know Mom, she doesn't really know how to cook Korean food." I felt terrible saying that to Grandma, as though I was betraying my mom. But I needed Grandma on my side.

"Yes, your mom not know too much. She make Mexican food and tacos," she said scornfully. I loved tacos, but I let that one slide.

"Okay. You have time on Friday? I pick you up after school and we go Korean store to go shopping, okay? Korean girl should learn how to make Korean food. Good idea!" She sounded almost happy.

"Okay, Grandma. I'll come home right away after school on Friday," I said. "Thanks."

"Friday, we make *kimbap*," she said and she hung up the phone.

CHAPTER 5

We unloaded all the groceries from Grandma's car in the dark. We had spent a good long time at the grocery store. Too long. I was super tired and hungry and we still had a lot of work to do.

"Kimbap," my grandmother started, as we walked into the kitchen, with our hands full of plastic grocery bags. "Everybody's kimbap little bit different."

"It's like sushi right?" I asked.

Grandma had a shocked look in her eyes. "No! Not like sushi! Aigoo! Sushi use vinegar in the rice. Not in kimbap," Grandma scolded. "Your mother not teach you anything! Korean in name only! Sushi is *Jap-an-ese*," Grandma said each syllable slowly and with emphasis. "You NOT Japanese." She pointed her finger at me.

I kept quiet. She muttered to herself some more in Korean, and I couldn't understand what she was saying, but sometimes all you need to hear is the tone in somebody's voice, no matter what the language, and it was pretty clear she was irritated with me. There was no use arguing with her. I was just going to pretend I never mentioned the word *sushi*.

I watched her lay out the ingredients. Sheets of dried seaweed, eggs, beef, carrots, spinach, yellow pickled radish. "You wash spinach. Wash very well." She bent down into a cabinet and pulled out a colander. "Then you wash carrots," Grandma ordered.

She proceeded to fry the beef she had bought at the store while I washed. I washed for a long time. I was afraid of doing it wrong. She had started a pot of water to boil and after I finally handed her the spinach she dumped it in the pot of boiling water. "Only one, two minutes," she instructed. Then she dumped the contents back into the colander in the sink. "You squeeze later, when cool." She moved on to the carrots, which she had started to slice into perfect long, slim sticks.

"Now, cook carrots." She gestured for me to come to the stove and help her. I took the wooden spoon. "Add little sesame oil, not too much!"

The preparation was endless. It was way past dinner time and I was so hungry, but I couldn't tell Grandma that. She was trying to help me, and I was kind of surprised at how nice she was being, especially after how I had stuck my foot in my mouth earlier.

We were finally ready to roll up the kimbap. We stood side by side, each with a sheet of seaweed laid out. "Now, spread rice. Not too thick." My grandmother showed me. We laid out each of the other ingredients we had prepared and finally, *finally*, we were ready to roll.

"Not bad for first roll." Grandma smiled as I finished rolling. "Next time, little bit tighter."

"Can I eat some now, Grandma?" I asked.

"Okay, I slice for you, but we still have to finish more."

She got out a big knife and sliced up the roll I had made. It was nearly 8pm, and after having been surrounded by food all afternoon, finally getting to eat it felt so good. I loved the way the pickled radish crunched in my mouth. I ate the whole roll very quickly.

"You want some soup too?" Grandma asked.

"Yes, please." She pulled out a pot from the fridge and set it on the stove for me. I didn't even care if it was tteokguk again. I was so hungry any soup would have been welcome.

"Let's finish, then soup is ready," she said as she popped a slice of the kimbap into her mouth. "Taste good. We did good job."

We rolled about ten more rolls together and she packaged most of it up for me to take home. It was very late when Grandma drove me home, but I had my rolls of kimbap in a plastic bag and I had actually had a good time with my grandmother.

As I was getting out of the car, Grandma said to me, "Tori says you have party next week?"

"Yes," I replied carefully. How did my grandmother know these things? Did she and Tori text each other?

"Okay, maybe I see you in a few days," she said. "Make sure your dad eats kimbap tonight. Best fresh."

I nodded. "Thanks, Grandma. I learned a lot today."

She nodded slightly and drove away leaving me standing at the curb with a bag full of food. I went into the house and put the food in the kitchen.

Then I barged into Tori's room. "Why did you tell Grandma that I have a party next week?" I asked angrily. I had answered Madison's email with my reply being "maybe," so it was not a sure thing that I was even going to go.

"Because," she got up off her bed, "I started to make you...this!" She pulled a dress out of her closet.

I was a little bit stunned. It was the Korean dress she had worn for Heritage Month, but it was totally mutilated.

"A shredded dress?" I asked.

"Ugh! I knew you wouldn't be able to appreciate it yet, so I was waiting to show you until I was closer to being done. But I guess Grandma spilled the beans. I was planning to use the traditional material but turn it into something more modern."

I had no vision for this kind of thing. A traditional Korean hanbok is brightly colored, like a box of bold pastel crayons. The fabric is very silky and smooth. But mostly, I have to say, it doesn't look that great. Something about the style and the colors just doesn't appeal to me. Japanese kimonos look beautiful, Chinese cheongsam dresses look elegant. Pretty much any other Asian traditional dress looks better than the one I was stuck with. Wearing a hanbok, you get all hot and stuffy. After a while, you look and feel like a big piece of sticky candy.

"You may as well do a preliminary fitting for me," she said.

"I'm confused," I said as I slipped the mangled dress over my head. "Is this dress for the Red Carpet Party or is this for my Heritage Month project?"

She shrugged. "Both. Why not?" she said, even though she had stuck a few pins in her mouth as she got to work. "I was just really inspired and I felt like making it. Hopefully you can use it for something," she said half talking, half spitting because of the pins.

"Did I mention that there's kimbap downstairs?" I said as I held my arms out while she pinned the sides of the dress.

"Oh, did Mom buy some at the store today?" she asked. She only had one pin left, so I could almost understand her now.

"No, Grandma and I made it," I said. "Where do you think I've been all afternoon and evening?"

"I don't follow your every move. Anyway, I was so busy making this dress, I lost track of time!"

"Ow!" I yelled. A pin stuck me in the ribs.

"Don't move!" Tori yelled at me.

"I love how I get hurt and it's somehow all my fault," I muttered.

"Okay, stay here, I'm going to go eat some kimbap really fast. It's best fresh." She ran out of her room and left me standing motionless. I was afraid to move because I didn't want to get stuck by a pin again.

Tori came back holding a small plate of kimbap and chewing. "You made this?" She pointed to her mouth. It didn't have any kimchi in it, so I guess it passed her fresh breath test.

"Yes. Well, I helped Grandma."

"It's good!" she said with her mouth still full of food. She may be the pretty one, but she didn't have the best manners. "Okay, take it off. I need to sew it now."

Very carefully I took off the dress and passed it to Tori. She had a little sewing machine set up on a table in her room and she started digging around looking for the right color of thread. I left her to her work. I knew she wanted to work in peace and quiet. As I opened the door to leave, she yelled, "Hey!"

I turned around.

"Take this plate downstairs and get me another roll, would you?" she said through a mouthful of food. When did my "beautiful" sister develop such gross habits?

"Say it, don't spray it," I said as I grabbed the plate out of her hands.

"Don't be a smart aleck." She finally swallowed and threw a loose piece of fabric at me. "I'm doing you a favor remember?"

Was she? I didn't remember asking her for help. I heard her sewing until late in the evening. When she gets an idea in her head, she really goes for it. I had to admire her determination.

CHAPTER 6

Tori gave me the dress the next day. She said, "I have something for you!"

I couldn't believe it had only taken her an evening to finish the dress. "Try it on!" she encouraged me.

Without any more needles and pins, it was easy to try on. I looked at myself in the mirror. Tori did a nice job on my Korean dress. I was pleasantly surprised by my sister. Lately she had actually been really nice to me and it was so much better than the moody teenager she had started to become. The dress, which traditionally is very wide and flowing, was tapered and more fitted. On the upper short jacket part, she had taken the sleeves in so that they didn't flop around so much.

"Mom!" Tori shouted downstairs. "Come see this!" I was standing in front of the mirror fussing when my mom came in.

"Tori, you did this?" my mom asked.

She looked pleased. "Yes, I did. Not bad, huh?"

"Tori, it looks amazing! I was wondering what you were doing last night. What's it for?"

"Krista's class project, or whatever."

"Krista, you look stunning in it!" my mom continued to gush.

"Well let's not get carried away, Mom. She still needs some work. You can't wear *this* dress with your hair in *that* ponytail." Tori flicked my hair. There she was. I had been wondering where the old Tori had gone.

The doorbell rang.

"I called Grandma to come see," Tori told me.

Grandma? Seriously? I hadn't even had my breakfast yet! My mom went to get the door. I started to panic. I didn't want her to see me. We had had a nice evening making kimbap, but I couldn't quite help the feeling that she would judge me and the dress, and she was never one to hold back what she had to say.

Tori saw the look in my eyes as I began to take off the dress. "No, keep it on. I already told her about it. Let her see, I think she might like it."

"She's going to be mean, Tori. She's mean to me. You wouldn't understand," I told her. "Also, she was pretty mad at me when I said kimbap was like sushi."

"Oh no, you didn't!" Tori said. "You offended Korean people around the globe!"

"Tori, I'm serious. Haven't you noticed? She just doesn't like me as much as she likes you."

"That's not true," she said.

"It IS!" I insisted. "Mom knows."

"Well, maybe it's because you don't take care of yourself," she said.

"What is *that* supposed to mean?" I said indignantly.

"Well, you know, you don't dress…"

"Like a girl?" I finished her sentence.

Tori paused awkwardly, because it was exactly what she was going to say, but she just couldn't find a nice way to say it.

"I am almost twelve years old!" I shouted. "I can wear whatever I want!"

"Listen Krista, Grandma is just a bit old-fashioned. She's an old Korean lady who hasn't really come to terms with the fact that she's not in Korea anymore. She likes things a bit more traditional, that's all," Tori said quietly.

We heard my mom bring her upstairs. I held my breath.

"You have to see this!" my mom said as she came down the hallway.

She came into my room, and I was frozen. Grandma stood still for a moment. It was silent for what felt like hours, but was probably only five seconds. "Tori, this is hanbok I gave you before?" she finally asked.

"Yes, Grandma," she answered.

She took a few steps toward me. "It was very expensive." She clicked her tongue at us, which was usually not a good sign. "Krista, turn around," she ordered.

I dutifully obliged, feeling very nervous.

Grandma lifted up her chin and looked at me through her glasses. "Krista, you got period yet? Your body change. Look not bad. But you need visit to salon. Hair is terrible. Grandma take you next weekend before party."

There were no words. Where was the giant hole that I could have curled up in? Could my grandmother make me feel any weirder? Was that supposed to be a compliment? I felt my entire body turn red with embarrassment. I didn't know it could do that. At least she didn't give me a chance to answer her.

"Not traditional dress. But looks a *little* Korean." She continued to stare at me in the dress. "You wear to your Chinese friend's party, she not know any better, but I not allow you to wear to Korean church or family wedding," she said.

She turned to Tori. "I think Tori you have good eye for clothes. You make even Krista look nice."

"Thanks, Grandma." Tori smiled and I saw her eyes dart sideways toward me. Did she believe me now?

"Thanks, Grandma." I fake smiled. Her compliments to me were always backhanded. I threw Tori an I-told-you-so stare.

CHAPTER 7

After we got back from school on Monday, my mom had made us pierogies. Tori took her plate and went to the living room to eat and talk on her phone with her friend, but I always liked to sit with my mom at the kitchen table. I loved it when she chopped up bacon and sprinkled it on top with sour cream and thinly sliced green onions.

As I settled in, she said, "I just got an email from Madison's mom about her birthday party on Saturday. She said Madison had already invited you, but this was more for me to know the time and date."

I stopped eating.

"She says you haven't confirmed yet. Why not?" my mom asked.

"Yeah, I got the email a few days ago, but I replied 'maybe,'" I said. "I guess I forgot about it."

"It sounds like fun. Getting all dressed up, right?" She looked at me hopefully. But even I could tell she was faking her enthusiasm. My mom was not one of those chipper, overly happy moms whose voices go an octave higher when talking to kids. Maybe she lost all her enthusiasm when she was a vice-principal.

"No, actually, it sounds horrible," I grumbled as I shoved a pierogi in my mouth.

"You haven't been to a party in a while, so I thought it wouldn't be the worst thing in the world."

"Mom, yes it would! You of all people know I don't like wearing dresses. And you know that I don't like people staring at me. I'm not Tori! Grandma and Tori think I can wear the hanbok. but I don't think it's appropriate. I can't go!" I sulked. The bacon didn't even taste good anymore.

"Why not?" she asked indignantly.

"Because it's not really something you'd wear on a Red Carpet—it's too Korean-looking," I tried to explain.

"Just because it's *Korean*-looking doesn't mean it's not appropriate for Madison's party. Sounds like the whole point of the party is to dress up in something out of the ordinary. Believe me, the dress Tori made is out of the ordinary."

I stared at my plate of pierogies. I chewed slowly, thinking hard. The party was in a few days and I didn't know what to do, so I pretended to forget about it.

Jason and I hadn't planned to meet up today after school, but I gave him a call at home to see what he was up to. I needed to think about other things.

"You want to do something?" I asked him when I got him on the phone.

"Sure. We're not doing much here in the nut house," he replied. I could hear dogs barking in the background. "But I am supposed to walk the dogs."

"Keep them on a short leash!" I said. I didn't like his dogs very much. One of them was super hyper. He was like a dog version of a child on too much sugar.

"Okay, okay," he said. I could tell he was smiling. "Meet me at the park behind school?"

"Okay, fifteen minutes," I said.

We hung up and I told my mom I was leaving. "Come back for dinner!" was all she said. I'm glad she finally started letting me out of the house by myself without fretting and worrying like she used to.

As I walked, I wondered what to do about the party. My mom was right, I hadn't been to too many parties lately. I wasn't sure if it was because we were all getting older and some of us (namely me) thought parties were kind of babyish, or maybe I just wasn't very popular. Jason was really the only person at school I spent a lot of time with. Once in a while we joined other kids in games, but not that often. Maybe nobody else liked me. Maybe I didn't like anybody else? Maybe it was time to take a chance. I could wear the dress Tori had made for me. It was pretty cool looking…

I was shaken out of my thoughts when I saw Jason being dragged behind the leashes of his dogs and I waved at him. He gestured to the field to tell me where he was going. He was carrying the drool-stick and the ball that his dogs loved chasing.

"Hi!" he yelled from across the field.

I jogged up to him. "Hi!" I said.

He took his dogs off leash and hurled the ball into the field.

I'm pretty sure some drool flung off the ball and hit me in the face.

"Gross, Jason! My face is wet with dog drool!" I said as I wiped.

"Oh, come on. That was my first throw. There's no drool yet," he said.

"Oh great, it's *stale* dog drool," I said as I wiped my face harder.

We both laughed and spent the rest of the time playing with the dogs.

CHAPTER 8

I had tried not to think about it or mention it, but somehow, Grandma remembered the day of the party. She kept her promise and she picked me and Tori up early Saturday morning and dragged me (Tori went quite willingly) to a Korean beauty salon downtown where they proceeded to roll my hair, spray it into a helmet, and do my makeup.

It was my first time at a nice salon. For my usual haircuts, my mom still took me to the kids' salon where I sat in a chair that looked like a throne. She said it was "cheap and reliable" and I would just have to go there until I didn't fit the throne anymore.

This placed smelled like ammonia, hairspray, and there was a whiff of kimchi in the air. Somebody had eaten it for breakfast. There were a lot of young Korean ladies, all speaking Korean, and it could have been a salon in Seoul, not Vancouver. Not that I'd ever been to Seoul, but I was just imagining. Grandma spoke to the receptionist and said a bunch of stuff I couldn't understand. One of the ladies gestured for me to come with her, and another lady took Tori.

"Grandma, what are they going to do?" I asked nervously.

She tsked her tongue at me. "Krista, let them do work. Stop asking questions."

I sat in a chair and they put a small drape around the front of my shirt, so I guessed makeup was first. The lady pulled open a few drawers and started to get ready.

"Could you *not* over-do the makeup?" I asked the makeup artist.

She gave me a funny look. I don't think she spoke English.

"Grandma, could you ask them to NOT turn me into a K-pop star?"

"K-Pop! Yes, good! Good!" The makeup artist nodded.

"What you mean K-Pop?" Grandma asked confused.

"No, no," I shook my head. "Not K-Pop! Only a little bit of makeup!" I said that super loud, as if shouting it was going to help the makeup artist understand. Just then, I wished I could speak some Korean. "Tori, I need your phone! It's a translation emergency!"

She was getting her hair cut so she tossed it to me. I typed in "Not too much makeup" into a translation app and the makeup artist read it and sighed. Grandma scolded me, "She is expert, Krista. You not expert in makeup. Let her do something nice. In Korea women very beautiful, not like here. Everybody so casual. Ugly boots and nobody take care to make their face."

I sighed. I had a feeling I wouldn't ever win any kind of argument with my grandmother in my entire life. I relented a little, but not completely, I still managed to give the hairdresser a hard time. I said "No" to just about everything she was trying to do. My grandmother kept tsking me with her tongue.

They had me turned around looking away from the mirror most of the time. After all my complaining, I think Grandma told them in Korean not to let me look at what they were doing because Tori's chair was facing the mirror.

After they were nearly done they finally turned my chair so I could see the mirror. I didn't recognize myself. It took my brain a while to register what it was seeing. I guess I looked nice, but it was hard to process the stranger looking back at me. It wasn't all together the worst thing that I had ever experienced, but I couldn't imagine spending all that time every day trying to look like that.

But for my sister, it was as if she had finally found herself. She looked like she was right out of one those calendars at the Korean market with those girls with perfect milky white skin and hair perfectly curled. She looked beautiful. They even put special tape on her eyelids to make her eyes look bigger. She could even have been on the cover of the Korean fashion magazine that we had flipped through while we were waiting.

Tori and I had regular Korean eyes. While we were looking through all the magazines in the salon, it became obvious that none of the models had eyes like ours. They all had these impossibly big round eyes. The tape changed the way Tori looked—suddenly, she had those eyes too.

The makeup lady asked me if I wanted to try it. Well, it was more like, she held up a sheet of eye tape, pointed to it, and then pointed to my eyes. I looked over at Grandma and Tori, and they both nodded their heads. It was for this party, so I agreed, very reluctantly. I closed my eyes, felt her touch my eyelids and when I opened up my eyes, the salon ladies gathered around me and started muttering stuff in Korean I didn't understand. But they were all smiling and nodding at me.

"They do nice job, right Krista? Your sister, so beautiful! In few years, I take you and Tori to Korea. You have *ssangapul* surgery. Big eyes. Even more pretty!" Tori beamed and Grandma patted her on the arm affectionately. She even squeezed my shoulder. It was the first time my grandmother had ever liked the way I looked. Of course, it was also the first time I didn't actually look like myself.

The ladies gave me and Tori some extra tape on our way out. We all bowed excessively as we left the salon and said our good-byes and thank-yous.

When we got home, my mom stared at me until I started to feel uncomfortable. "What? Why are staring at me?" I asked.

"Just wondering about all the makeup," she said and gestured to my eyes. "Do you like it?"

"Well," I started, "it's okay, I guess."

"Is that tape?" She peered at my eyes.

"Well, it's not regular tape, it's the special eye tape," I answered.

"Does it feel weird?" she asked.

I shrugged. Then I noticed something for the first time. My mom had double-eyelids.

"Do you wear the tape?" I asked her.

"No." She looked at me, confused. "Krista, I hardly ever wear makeup and I certainly don't bother with tape on my eyes."

"But you have the double-eyelids," I said.

"Well, I was just born with them." She shrugged. "Honestly, honey, I've never really thought a lot about it."

Huh, easy for her to say. Her eyes were really big, why did I have such small eyes? Why had I never noticed before?

"Ready to go soon?" she asked.

"I just need to get the dress on. Give me two more minutes." I ran upstairs.

"Be careful of hair and makeup!" Grandma shouted at me as I ran up the stairs.

After dressing, I looked at myself in a full-length mirror. Who was I? It didn't look like me. I really couldn't tell if I loved it or if I hated it. I went downstairs as quickly as I could and said to my mom, "Come on, let's go. I think the party has started already." I ignored my sister and grandmother and went outside and waited by the car.

My mom came out and I could see Tori and Grandma standing by the window watching us.

My mom was quiet while we were driving and luckily Madison's house wasn't very far. She had a small smirk on her face the entire time. She parked the car, but I didn't move.

"Get in there already." She practically shoved me out of the car. "You look nice, Krista. But I want you to remember that this is still just a party. It's fun and make believe. Don't take it too seriously."

I wasn't really sure what she meant, but nodded anyway.

Walking up to Madison's house, I felt very self-conscious. I kept pulling at my dress, fidgeting with the fabric, reminding myself to breathe.

I rang the doorbell, and I could already hear voices inside the house.

Madison opened the door. She was wearing a long pink ball gown, and on her head was a very large tiara.

She paused to stare at me for a second before she shrieked, "Krista! Oh my gosh you look sooooooo cool!" She turned around and continued to shriek, "Everybody come look at Krista! She looks awesome!"

I was suddenly surrounded by all these girls from my class, but it didn't feel real because there was so much taffeta and puffiness.

Can you say *awkward*? All the girls were staring at me, asking me questions and touching my dress. I heard a lot of "Oh wow!" and "Oh my God!" around me. It felt like a hundred pairs of eyes were on me. They were asking me five thousand questions all at once. But the general feeling of approval in the room meant that they liked my dress. I finally relaxed and went into the house, ready to enjoy myself.

Madison had invited almost all the girls in our class, and everybody came as dressed up as they possibly could manage. Most looked like they had raided their mom's closets, and my dress sure looked the most unique. In addition to being a "Red Carpet" party, it was also a spa party. We were all getting our nails done. I had already had my hair and makeup done before the party, thanks to Grandma.

I had been so worried about the party and the dress that Tori had designed, but it was okay after all. Maybe even better than okay.

I watched as some of the girls got their nails done before me. It was a nice little setup. Three ladies had on these short white jackets. It reminded me of my dad's lab coat for work, but more stylish. They had little tables with a bright light and a display of nail polishes and we could all pick a color. There were clean white towels stacked neatly on their tables next to some supplies like scissors and files. All the girls were giddy—there was a lot of nervous and excited laughter in the air.

Madison went first of course, since it was her party. She picked a soft pink color to match her soft pink dress. I was happy to wait to see what the other girls were picking. When it wasn't your turn for nail polish, Madison's mom had set up a dancing video game for us to play, but I was not about to get any hotter, so I just stood around watching girls get their nails done.

When it was my turn for my nail polish, I picked a nice bright red and I think I even almost smiled. Madison sat down on a stool next to me. "I'm so glad you came to my party Krista! You look really cool!"

"Thanks," I replied shyly. She got up to go talk to other people.

Emma walked by and whispered, "Krista, you have the coolest dress here. So amazing. Your dress is even better than Madison's! Don't tell her I said that!"

I smiled. "Don't worry, I won't."

"That's a good color choice," Emma continued as she pointed down to my nails. "It goes really well with your dress."

Even though I was used to hanging out with boys, well, actually just one boy, it was surprisingly fun to spend some time with Madison and all the other girls. I had spent years going to school with them, but honestly, couldn't really say that I knew them very well. I can't say I was totally involved in a lot of the conversation or dancing, I mostly just watched and listened, but it was a better time than I had thought it was going to be. I was disappointed when it was time to go home.

CHAPTER 9

The next day at school Jason asked me, "So, how was it?"

"How was what?" I said.

"The *party*." He slapped my arm. "Stop pretending you don't know what I'm talking about! That's all I can hear the girls talking about. Everybody's dresses. Especially yours. I heard from Emma that it was a real hit."

I shrugged. "I guess it was okay."

"I thought it looked nice."

I stopped cold. "How do you know?"

"Emma showed me a picture." He flashed his phone at me, and there I was looking at myself.

Marcus, who in addition to being the worst yoga student in our class was also the most obnoxious boy in our class, happened to be looking over our shoulders and said, "Whoa Krista, you wore a dress?! You look kind of nice! I am totally shocked!"

"Get lost, Marcus!" I shouted at him and chased him away.

It was so weird. One party and one dress, and suddenly I felt like people had noticed me for the first time in years.

Madison interrupted us as I was getting rid of Marcus. "Krista, you want to come hang out by the tree with us at lunch?"

The tree. It was a big old cherry tree with a big crack in the trunk. It was far off in the corner of the grassy area near the school. Those girls, Madison and her best friends, protected that tree like it dropped golden apples. The entire school knew that it was *their* tree and they would force you away from it. Nobody else could even come near it. It had been like that for as long as we could remember. Jason and I always joked that they performed voodoo under that tree.

"Uh, I don't know Madison. Jason and I usually hang out near the field," I said.

"It's okay, Krista. I can go watch the basketball game at lunch," Jason said. I looked at him to figure out if he was for real. He hated basketball.

"Great," Madison said. "See you there. Don't bring anybody else. It's by invitation only." She turned around on her shiny ballet flats and walked away.

"Oooohhh!" Jason said. "You've been invited to the tree. They must have really liked your dress this weekend."

I stared down at my beat up running shoes and wondered why. My red nail polish from this weekend had already chipped away. I certainly didn't look like I fit in with those girls today. I was dressed like my normal self.

The rest of the morning I couldn't concentrate because I knew lunchtime was coming soon. I tried very hard to pay attention in math, but I wasn't doing a good job of it. When lunch finally did come, my tuna wrap was tasteless and my tortilla was kind of wet and gooey. Not my mother's best lunch effort.

We packed up our lunch kits after we heard the bell that Jason and I referred to as the get-the-heck-out-of-here bell. That meant it was time to head outside for the rest of the lunch hour. Madison stopped near me in the cloakroom and said, "Coming?"

"Uh, sure," I said as I put on my jacket.

I looked at Jason and he said, "I'll see you later." He smiled awkwardly as he put his hand on my shoulder. I watched him walk away and I didn't feel good.

I was feeling totally nervous. I tried to tell myself I was being silly, but as I walked next to Madison, she was soon surrounded by her usual group of friends: Emma, Cassie, and Arden. Halfway down the hall, Emma noticed that I seemed to be tagging along behind them. She stopped talking and stared at me before Madison noticed and said, "Oh it's okay. I invited her." Emma shrugged and continued talking as we reached the bottom of the stairs.

I took a deep breath and followed the girls to the tree.

CHAPTER 10

After lunch our class headed to the library to continue working on our Heritage Month projects. I didn't have too much research to do, but I decided it would be a good idea if I pretended to be busy. Some people headed to desks, but most went to a computer.

Once we were settled at our table, Jason leaned over and whispered, "So what *really* goes on at that tree?" We hadn't had a chance to talk since lunch ended, and I was so thankful he came over to talk to me.

I smiled and whispered back, "I'll never tell."

"Oh come on!" he said.

"Okay, okay, I'll give you a hint." I looked around to make sure nobody was listening. "It's actually pretty boring. They talk about their favorite singers and who's cute and who's not."

He stared at me in disbelief. "That's it?" He sounded disappointed.

"For real, that's it."

"I'm underwhelmed," he said. "I thought for sure they hid voodoo dolls under their jackets and cursed people they didn't like."

I smiled. "I wish I had a better story for you. They are actually okay. I didn't know some of the singers or actors they were talking about, and they found it hard to believe that I didn't have my own phone, but it wasn't terrible."

I looked around before I continued. "But, I will let you in on one very interesting fact."

He leaned in. "Tell me!"

"Arden has a huge crush on Marcus," I said with eyes wide open.

"Ew," Jason replied, looking repulsed.

"I know!" I said. It felt good to talk to him this way again. Just one lunch break away from him had felt weird, especially because I knew he was there at school, not home sick, but we both seemed fine. Turns out we didn't have to spend *every* minute at school together.

The next couple of days at school were pretty normal. Madison and her friends were talking to me more, and trying to include me in things. They asked me to come hang out with them again at lunch on Tuesday, but I had a good excuse this time, because Jason and I were office monitors and I couldn't join them. It felt nice to be included. I hadn't ever really noticed that I wasn't included before. I mean I wasn't a social outcast, people were never mean to me, but I just wasn't ever considered.

The next time we were in the library, I ended up next to Emma on a computer and she started to talk to me about very random things. She told me about her older sister, who apparently knew Tori. I was just listening to her talk, when Mrs. June walked by so Emma stopped. That was okay because I had to really think about how to make my presentation work. I needed to stop gossiping and start working. How did these girls get anything done? They talked endlessly!

I stared out the window for a while wondering how I could make my random ideas for my project come together. Grandma had already taught me how to make kimbap, but how was I going to hand that in? I was staring at a blank sheet of paper next to my computer screen when Madison walked by and passed me a note. I opened it very slowly. It said, "Can you come to my house after school Wednesday?"

Actually I could, kind of, but it was a Wednesday and usually Jason and I hung out at my house on Wednesdays. It had been like that for years. It was just understood. I closed the paper and put it in the back pocket of my jeans.

I looked at the table behind me. Jason had seen everything. He looked at me and made a what-was-that? gesture, but I just shook my head and pretended to be busy.

It was kind of weird. I didn't feel that Madison and I had hit it off under the tree, but maybe I just didn't know how to read other people very well. I did mostly just hang out with Jason all the time, and he wasn't anything like them, so I didn't really have a good reference point.

I got up to go to the washroom and Madison followed me. "So can you?" she asked as we walked down the hallway.

"Uh, Jason usually comes over on Wednesdays," I said.

"So? Ditch him. He won't care, he's just a boy," Madison said. "Why do you two spend so much time together anyway?"

"He's been my best friend since preschool," I said quietly.

"Well, things change and people grow up," she said matter of factly. "Just come at 3:30, okay? You remember where I live, right?"

"Okay," I said, walking into a stall. As I locked the door, I wondered how Jason would take it.

After school, he waited outside the classroom door for me, as he normally does, and I nervously asked him if it would be okay if I went to Madison's house. He looked a little surprised, but then said, "Sure, Krista. It's okay if we miss one Wednesday, right? I'll see you later."

Then he turned and left quickly. I was taken aback at how quickly he left. We usually walked home together, at least as far as we could before he headed off toward his house. Was he mad? I couldn't tell. He said it was fine, so I guess he was okay with it.

When I got home, my mom was not so understanding.

"Where's Jason?" she asked.

"Um, he's not coming today because Madison invited me to her house after school," I said. "I talked to him about it at school and he said it was no problem."

"Red Carpet Party Madison?" she asked.

"Yes, her."

"So why couldn't you go a different day? Wednesday is when Jason comes over. It's been like that for years, right?" she said.

"Mom," I said, irritated. "Jason doesn't have to come over *every* Wednesday you know."

She paused. "I know, you're right, he doesn't have to, but he just *does*. Plus, I made muffins for him, I mean for both of you." She pointed to a platter on the counter with freshly made lemon and blueberry muffins.

Jason did like my mom's muffins. My heart sank a little bit at the thought of him missing out on them.

But it was only *one* Wednesday. My mom was making such a big deal out of it.

"Well, you can pack some in my lunch tomorrow and I'll give them to him, okay?"

Tori came in with her headphones on and said loudly, "Where's your boyfriend?"

I had had enough. Jason said it was fine, so why was everybody making me feel bad about it? I stomped out of the room. "Bye! I'll call later!" I shouted, as I got ready to go to Madison's house.

"What?" Tori said to my mom, looking confused as she took off her headphones. "It is Wednesday, right?"

"Touchy subject, I guess," I heard my mom say.

CHAPTER 11

Maybe it was because I had never been to Madison's house alone before, but it was so strange to be there. The party had been crazy with lots of people around and the house had been decorated. Now that it was just a normal day at her house, I finally got a good look around her bedroom. I scanned my eyes around the room trying not to make it obvious that I was staring at everything.

Was this a cotton candy parallel universe? She had a lot of pink stuff in her room. A lot. Her curtains were pink, her walls were pink, and her bedding was all pink and frilly. There were stuffed animals all over the place. I didn't know what to make of it. I actually didn't know what to make of her.

I'm a girl—why did other girls confuse me so much? Tori was definitely confusing, but I hadn't realized that my classmates were too. I felt so different from Madison. I wasn't sure why I was even there. She was all "mature" at school and seemed so sophisticated, but here in her room, she just seemed like a little kid.

"I also invited Emma and Arden, okay?" she told me when I got there. "But they have dance until 4:30, so they'll come after."

"Okay," I said. I was feeling totally awk- ward. I just stood around her room, not really knowing where to sit or what to look at.

"Here, sit on this," she offered, generously throwing me a lifeline. I think it was called a pouf. I read about them in a design magazine at my dentist's office last month.

"Thanks," I said. I was suddenly very aware about the way I was dressed. I had on jeans—I almost always wore jeans—and a plain navy blue t-shirt. My hair was in its usual ponytail. I took a very hard look at Madison, and saw she was wearing designer yoga pants that were probably never used for yoga (this is Vancouver, everybody wears yoga pants) and an off-the-shoulder t-shirt that didn't look nearly as boring as mine.

"What do you want to do?" she asked. I noticed she had a TV in her room, a computer, a tablet, and a cell phone. Her parents were clearly not as strict about electronics as mine.

I didn't think she'd be into playing cards like I did with Jason, so I shrugged. "Want to watch TV?" I suggested. At least I wouldn't have to think of things to talk about. I never knew making new friends was so awkward. I was looking forward to Emma and Arden coming over later so we'd have somebody else around.

Madison's mom poked her head into the room. "Sorry girls, I forgot to ask if you wanted a snack."

I sat up, excited at the thought of eating something. I'd forgotten to eat at my house before I came here and my stomach was rumbling. I really should have grabbed one of my mom's muffins.

"No thanks," Madison said. "We're fine. Go away!"

My shoulders drooped and I sat back on the pouf. I guess food wasn't a big priority at this house. I hoped she wouldn't hear my stomach.

"You know what I noticed?" Madison asked as she sat up straight.

"No, what?" I answered.

"Your eye makeup looked really cool the day of my party," she said.

"Oh, that was mostly tape," I answered.

"Tape?"

"Yeah, like special eye tape they make in Korea," I said.

"You looked really good with it. You should think about wearing it to school more," she told me. "Korea has such an amazing fashion scene, you know."

"Oh thanks. I saw a bunch of Korean magazines in the salon and the style is so different, isn't it?" I tried my best to make "small talk." I admit it wasn't easy for me. Like when was the last time I talked to Jason about fashion? Never. I suddenly wondered if she was going to ask me if I wanted to put makeup on with her, but luckily, she pulled out some magazines instead.

"Look at these!" She happened to have some Korean magazines, which surprised me. "Of course

I can't read any of these, but I like to look at the pictures. Can you read any of it?"

"No, not a single word. My parents don't even read or speak Korean."

We flipped through the pages and talked about what we saw—that dress looks nice, or that hairstyle looks weird, that kind of stuff—until Arden and Emma came. Time passed more quickly than I expected. I realized that with Jason, we did active things together, but with these girls, I was sitting around talking about stuff. Lounging around and gossiping. It was all new to me.

The girls had a lot to talk about so I hoped it wasn't obvious that I was just listening and not actually joining the conversation most of the time. We laughed a lot because Arden has this very dramatic streak and likes to tell stories. Maybe I misjudged the girls. I always assumed that they were kind of mean and snobby, but when you spent time with them, they were pretty nice.

When it was time to go home, my mom picked me up.

When I got into the car she said, "Did you have a good time?"

"Yeah, I did," I replied, and my mom looked surprised.

"Oh." She paused. "Well, I guess that's great!" She sounded a little *too* happy to be real. She wasn't normally that perky.

We drove home the rest of the way in silence, which was good, because I had a bit of a headache. Those girls could sure talk a lot and I wasn't used to it. I was so hungry that when I came home to the smell of chicken souvlaki, I think I literally drooled.

"I left a plate for you in the oven," my mom said. "Tori and I ate just before I came to pick you up, and your dad's not home yet."

I sat down with my mom at the table and started eating.

"Hungry?" she asked, almost laughing. "I've never seen you eat so quickly!"

"Yes," I said with a mouthful of chicken. "Madison and her family don't seem to eat."

"Well, every family has a different way of doing things," my mom said. She got up and squeezed my shoulder.

After I ate, I went upstairs because I wanted to lie down. I noticed that Tori had left a big bag full of clothes in my room.

"Tori!" I yelled. "What's this bag doing here?"

She popped her head into my room. "I've cleaned out my closet. Keep what you want and I'll get rid of the other stuff."

I realized that Tori had way nicer clothes than I did. On the top of her pile, designer yoga pants, similar to the ones Madison had on today. Why did I have "practical" clothes and how did Tori get all this nice stuff? I needed to talk to my mother about this situation. It was obviously not fair.

I spent the next hour or so trying on clothes. There were a bunch of clothes in her pile that fit me and that I liked. Tori walked in as I was trying on a plaid shirt. She tilted her head to the side as if she were thinking hard. "That one is okay on you, but you can't wear your usual jeans," she stated.

"What's wrong with my usual jeans?" I asked.

"The leg. Bootcut. Nobody wears bootcut any-more, unless you're a cowboy. A real cowboy, not a fake Western look. You're too Korean-looking, you can't pull off a Western look. You need skinny jeans," she said as she walked over to the pile of clothes and sorted through them until she found what she was looking for.

"Here." She held out some jeans. "These are too short for me now, but they should fit you. Try them on."

I paused.

"What, afraid to let me see your underwear? Geez, fine I'll turn around," she said.

I waited for her to physically turn around before I took off my jeans and put on her old pair.

"Can I turn around now?" she asked.

"Yes."

"See, that's better," she said as she looked at me with a critical eye. "But don't wear your usual running shoes."

Seemed like nothing I had was right. "What should I wear then?" I asked.

She rummaged through her pile some more. "If you're going to wear running shoes, at least let them be somewhat cool." She handed me what I guess she thought were "cool-looking" running shoes. I put those on too. I looked at myself in the mirror. I had to admit my sister had a better sense of fashion than I did.

I decided to wear Tori's old clothes to school the next day. No point leaving them in the bag on the floor.

"Thanks, Tori," I said.

"Sure." She nodded at me and got up to leave my room.

I had a lot to learn—about everything. I'm glad Tori could help me a little with clothes at least. I'm sure she had a few things to teach me about how to deal with other girls too.

The next morning, I stood in my bathroom for a while and pulled out the sheet of eye tape the ladies at the salon had given me. It just looked like a sheet of rounded stickers. I carefully peeled off a piece, leaned over the sink and tried to put a piece on my eyelid. I stepped back and looked at myself. I looked like somebody had punched me and my right eye was swelling. I didn't do it right. I ripped it off. I needed to practice more. Maybe now was not the right time. I didn't want to be late for school or get puffy eyes from continuously ripping off eyelid tape. I changed gears and decided to get dressed instead.

I put on the same outfit Tori seemed to approve of the night before, and my mom didn't say anything when I came downstairs, but I did catch her looking at me an extra-long time. I was waiting for her to say something, but she never did.

The girls at school all seemed to notice something different. Emma said, "Krista, I like what you're wearing today!" and Madison said, "Nice shirt!"

Nobody had ever complimented my clothing before. Was I really so different? "Thanks," I said, slightly embarrassed. "This is all Tori's old stuff."

At recess, they asked me to join them by the tree again. Jason heard and just kind of gave me a wry grin, like he was saying, go ahead, so I said okay. It was the fourth time in the past week that we had not hung out at school together. It felt weird, but he seemed okay with it. I walked with the girls to the tree and scanned my eyes around for Jason in the field. I could see he had found Marcus and Evan, and they were standing in the part of the field where Jason and I usually hung out. It looked like they were laughing.

CHAPTER 12

On the weekend, Dad was going to take me and Tori to the movies. The only problem was his car. It only had two seats.

"Alice, I need to borrow your car later," my dad told my mom while she drank her morning coffee and read the newspaper.

"Why? Something wrong with yours?" she asked.

"No, it's just movie day, remember? I'm supposed to take the girls to the movies this afternoon."

My mom put down her newspaper and looked at my dad with her blank stare. "Oh right," she said sarcastically. "You have that ridiculous car with only TWO seats and a manual transmission that I can't drive. I remember now."

"Alright, alright," my dad muttered.

"What if I have stuff to do?" My mom was giving Dad a hard time. I watched silently, eating my bowl of cereal. They went through this same routine every time my dad needed to take more than one person in his car. I think my mom loved tormenting him sometimes.

"Can you do your stuff now then? I want to take them to a show in the early afternoon."

"Don't you wish you had a car that could actually carry the entire family?" Mom put her coffee cup in the sink. "Fine, I'll go do my errands now."

She left to go do whatever moms do on Saturday mornings and so it was just me and my dad at the kitchen table.

"She really hates your car, huh?" I said, chewing my last mouthful of cereal.

"Yes, Krista, yes she does." My dad opened the newspaper to the sports section.

Tori finally came downstairs. It was almost 9am. She rubbed her head and said, "Where's Mom?"

"She left to do some errands," my dad answered.

"Did she leave me any breakfast?" Tori asked.

"No," I answered as I put my bowl in the sink.

"I'll make you something," my dad offered.

Tori rolled her eyes. "I can pour my own bowl of cereal, Dad." She reached into the cupboard for a bowl.

"So, it's movie day!" My dad tried to sound cheerful.

"Oh God..." Tori sighed as her shoulders slumped.

"What, too cool to spend some time with your dad?" he asked her as she poured the milk.

"Well actually, yes," she answered after swallowing her first spoonful.

"It'll be fun!" He gave her shoulder a playful push.

"No, Dad, no it won't."

And Tori was right, the movie wasn't very fun. My dad hated parking my mom's minivan so he always ended up parking as far away from the main entrance as possible, even though there were lots of spots close by. When we got there, the movie I wanted to see was sold out, so we ended up seeing this dumb movie about a dumb teenage girl who falls in love with a dumb boy (Tori's pick). Blah. Then my dad let me eat way too much popcorn (sore belly). On the way home he told us that we had to go to Grandma's house for dinner (surprise!).

We picked up my mom, who had been at home all afternoon. "So girls," Mom greeted us as she got into the car. "How was the movie?"

Tori shrugged her shoulders. I said, "Meh."

"What? Just *meh*? Personally, I thought it was terrible," my dad said. This was my dad trying to be funny.

"It was okay. The actor was cute," said Tori.

I rolled my eyes. My mom was turned in her seat looking at us. She smiled. "Off to Grandma's house," Dad said as we drove off.

It was still only 4pm, and after my giant bag of popcorn, I had no interest in eating dinner at all.

We piled out of the minivan and Grandma greeted us at the door with a big smile. once we were in her house, she pulled me aside and said, "Krista, you help with *japchae*."

I was put in charge of washing and slicing vegetables. My grandmother opened a drawer in her kitchen and said, "I bought you apron," as she put it over my head. "Remember how to squeeze spinach?" How could I forget?

"Yes, Grandma, I remember. Thank you for the apron, it's nice."

"Okay, squeeze." She slid a bowl of blanched spinach my way. I took it and went to the sink. I heard my dad turn on the TV in the living room. I heard Tori talking on her phone. My mom asked, "Can I help?"

"No, Krista can do," Grandma answered.

"Okay." Mom smiled at me and went to watch TV with Dad.

"After squeeze, put spinach in bowl with noodles," my grandmother instructed. "Slice mushrooms now. I do beef." She fired up her stovetop.

After we had finished preparing all the ingredients we assembled the japchae. It was one of my favorite dishes. Chewy noodles mixed with vegetables and sliced beef. It was good warm or room temperature. She served it with the usual table full of other side dishes, rice and there seemed to always be some kind of meat. Today she had stir-fried spicy pork.

"Thank you for preparing such a wonderful dinner," my mother said to Grandma before we started eating.

"Thanks, Mom, it looks delicious," my dad agreed.

Grandma looked very satisfied and smiled, as she looked around at all of us. I reluctantly picked up my chopsticks.

"Tori!" Grandma proclaimed. "Eat more!" Tori had been pushing noodles around her plate for a few minutes before Grandma had finally noticed.

"Grandma, I'm just not hungry. We had all this popcorn at the movie theater this afternoon and—"

"Alice! You spoil their appetites!" my grandmother started to scold. My mom shot my dad a cold look.

"Actually, Mom, it was me," my dad confessed.

She started muttering things in Korean as she got up from the table. My mother was still staring at my dad who just shrugged his shoulders. Grandma started rifling through her cabinets.

"I pack up for you to take home. Eat later," she said. turning to Tori. She had started to assemble empty plastic containers for leftovers. We never got away from Grandma's without at least some food. I was trying my best to eat, because I knew how she was about food. She made it, we were supposed to eat it. The pork was so spicy today that I needed four glasses of water with dinner, but I didn't want her to stare at me the way she stared at Tori for not eating. I was on the verge of being sick.

I put on a good enough show to satisfy her, so I was allowed to go lie down on the sofa. Which I did. My dad joined me and then undid his belt and the button of his pants. He put his head back on the sofa and gave me his death-by-food face and we both giggled.

CHAPTER 13

During our PE classes, we had been doing a dance unit. Normally I liked PE. I was a pretty good athlete without trying too hard. I wasn't the best at anything, but I wasn't the worst either. But this was a Hip Hop Dance unit. Mrs. June had got it into her head that she wanted us to perform at the Celebration of Dance that the school board put on once a year. She said her niece performed in it last year and she was so inspired that she wanted us to do it this year. So every PE class for the next few weeks, we were supposed to work on this dance. She even hired a local dance troupe to choreograph it. Mrs. June was serious. Madison, Arden, Cassie, and Emma were very good dancers, so they loved the idea of the whole Celebration of Dance. Me? Not so much.

My mom had put me in a ballet class when I was three. I guess she thought it would be cute. There are a lot of pictures of me in my little pink get-up before the class started, but—I don't remember this, this is just what my mom tells me—once the class started, I wouldn't listen to the teacher. Instead I just wanted to run around in a circle shouting. My mom couldn't quiet me down. She tells me that I ripped off my tutu and threw it at the teacher. She was too embarrassed to take me back for more classes. That was the end of my ballet and dance career.

I've seen all those videos of K-Pop stars doing awesome and amazing dance moves, so I can't blame having no rhythm on being Korean. Instead, I blame my dad. Hey, he brings it on himself by being a workaholic. It's easy to blame the absentee parent for all your failings. But if you have ever seen my dad dance, you'd agree that I most certainly got my lack of rhythm from him.

The choreographer, Denise, was super edgy. She wore her long hair straight down her back and her baseball cap backwards. She tied a plaid shirt around her waist and her black jeans had ripped up knees. The first couple of weeks she taught us some basic moves, but this week we were working on choreographing the whole class to run around the stage in formations using those basics. She shouted, "How many boys and how many girls in the class?"

We all looked around confused and nobody answered her, I think we were all a bit intimated by her cool factor.

"Okay, never mind. Boys on the left side of the stage, girls on the right!" she shouted when nobody gave her an answer.

"Your *other* left, boys!" She didn't even need a microphone. She herded us like cattle to count us off.

She came up on the stage and counted. "Perfect! An even number!"

"Partner up!" she shouted. "One boy, one girl! Go!"

Of course there was awkward jostling with nervous glances and hesitant moves to potential partners. I just automatically headed over to Jason who saw me coming, and he then turned around and asked Cassie. Cassie! I stopped dead in my tracks. He didn't even look back at me.

Marcus then tapped me on the shoulder. I let out a big sigh. Everybody else had already partnered up.

"Boys! Two lines! Line up with your partners to your right! Girls grab your partner's hand!" More stage jostling and then I reluctantly grabbed Marcus' clammy hand once the line had formed. I was so mad. How could Jason leave me to partner up with Marcus?

It was hard to listen to Denise and pay attention because I was so angry. Or was I hurt? Whatever I was, my lack of ability to focus caused Denise to yell, "Girl with long black hair!" more than once. It was startling to realize that she meant me. Marcus even chided me, "Come on Krista, pay attention!" When the class clown is giving you a lecture about paying attention, you know you've lost it. By the end of the class, I was hot with rage and perspiration.

Today was the first day in years that I hadn't put my hair in a ponytail. Tori said it was time to change things up a little and she had urged me to try my hair loose. Big mistake. I was so hot by the end of PE that I was cursing my sister and her fashion suggestions. I also wore her old booties, again, her suggestion, and my feet were killing me! I would have given anything for my old comfy running shoes.

But after taking a long drink at the water fountain, and splashing some cool water behind my neck, I took five deep breaths. Mrs. June's breathing exercises were coming in handy, and I could feel my anger die down a little. I thought hard as I walked slowly back to class.

I suddenly remembered that *I* was the one who had been spending time with other people. Jason had seemed okay about everything, but then I started to remember a few little things over the last week and I realized maybe he wasn't okay. I had to show Jason that I still wanted to be his friend. I tried my very best not to hold a grudge against him or be mad for not choosing me as his dance partner. But, wow, it was hard. I was stuck with Marcus!

Since Jason and I had missed out on two of our Wednesdays and we hadn't been spending too much time together at school, I really wanted to make a point of making sure he was coming over today. It was obvious that we needed to reconnect. We needed our Wednesdays back. Before, it would have been a given, we wouldn't have even have had to talk about it. But today, we *had* to talk about it.

"Jason, you're coming today, right?" I asked him in the cloakroom after school as we all got our things ready to go home.

"Oh, is today Wednesday?" he asked. He didn't seem his usual self. He kept looking at his cloakroom hook, and not me.

"Yes," I said.

"Yeah, I guess I can come over for a while," he said. "But I told Marcus I'd go to his house later to help him with his project." Okay that one hurt a little. He had made other plans.

We walked to my house without saying too much. It was the first time I had ever felt awkward around him. We had been friends since we were *three* and it had never been so weird between us before. But when we got to the front door, I could see him smile. Jason took a deep breath as he entered the kitchen.

"I smell chocolate chip cookies!"

My mom smiled as she walked over to the fridge to get the milk. "Yes, good timing! Still warm, but not so hot they will burn your mouth."

She poured us each a glass of milk, and reached for two plates as we sat down. "What's new today? What were you two up to?" I'm glad she didn't say anything about not having seen him for a while.

"Krista hung out with Emma, Arden, Cassie, and Madison again today," Jason said before I took a sip of milk. "Under the cherry tree."

My mom looked surprised. "Really? I thought they had some kind of no boys rule."

"I didn't go, Mrs. Kim. Just Krista," he answered. He didn't look at me. I had the distinct impression that he was ratting me out to my mom.

My mom looked even more surprised, and then stared at me and tilted her head to the side.

"So what do these girls do under that tree?" she asked. Jason stopped eating and waited to hear.

"Well…" I started, "they were trying to work out a dance routine, you know, because they were pretty inspired by the whole Celebration of Dance idea." They both sat quietly listening. "But they couldn't agree on how to finish. Madison wanted to do a pyramid, and be on top, because she's the smallest. But Arden and Emma refused to get their knees dirty. So they just wanted a new opinion, you know? Like sometimes you just need fresh eyes. That's what they said. So, they did the routine for me and asked me what I thought would look good."

"But you don't like dancing," my mom said.

"But I wasn't actually doing the dancing! I was like the choreographer," I stated.

"So what did you suggest?" Jason asked.

"Well, Emma and Arden didn't want to get their knees dirty, that was the big problem, so I came up with a solution. I told them to squat, face each other, because it looked stupid with them squatting and facing forward, put their hands on their knees and one leg a bit further back so it looked good and Madison could be in the middle, standing with her arms in the air. So it looked like the same shape as a pyramid, but it actually *wasn't* a pyramid. Get it?"

My mom and Jason didn't say anything for a long time. I caught my mom glancing at Jason, as if she was trying to read his mind. In my head, I had time to rethink what I had just said aloud. It sounded a tiny bit lame, didn't it? It didn't feel lame when it was happening though.

"Was it fun to be with them?" my mom asked.

"Well, it was okay, I guess."

"What did you do today while this was happening Jason?" my mom asked.

He took another big bite of cookie and shrugged. "Not much. I found some of the boys in our class. They were making a pile of dirt, so I helped. Then I talked to Marcus a bit."

We ate in silence for a while. Awkward. So now my mom knew that Jason and I hadn't been the same as usual at school. Time to talk about something else.

"Mom?" I asked, desperate to change the subject.

"Yes?"

"I've been thinking more about my assignment. I need to ask Grandma if she'll come to school with me to make some Korean dishes for the class."

"Oh." She pursed her lips. "Could I help with it?"

"Well, Mom, no offense, but you're not exactly an expert in Korean food," I said.

"What do you mean?" My mom sounded offended.

"Well, like, do you even make your own kimchi?"

"No…" she started, "but that's because Grandma can be very critical. I'd rather she not be smug about it if my kimchi isn't as good at hers."

"So that's why I need to ask Grandma. She's the expert," I said.

"I'm sure Grandma will help you. She'd do any-thing for you girls," my mom said. "But still, make sure to ask her politely for her help."

"This is for our project?" Jason asked.

"Yes," I answered.

"Like I suggested a while ago?" he asked with a satisfied look in his eye.

"Yes, I guess you did mention it, didn't you? But I have some other ideas, too. I want to hand in some-thing on paper, like a booklet, after Grandma and I make food for the class."

"Do you want to ask her to prepare some food at home and then bring it to class?" my mom asked.

"No, I don't think so. I think we need to actually make it, in the class. Like the whole process. But it will be kind of tricky because there is no kitchen in the classroom, so I still have to figure it out," I said. "I'd like to ask her in person. She's not the easiest person to talk to on the phone. Is she coming here, or are we going there soon?"

"I'll call her over for dinner tomorrow, how about that?" my mom asked.

"Okay," I agreed.

"You two done your snack?"

"Yes, thank you, Mrs. Kim. Your cookies were delicious," Jason said as he put away his plate and cup into the sink. Polite as always. "I have to go, though. I promised Marcus."

It felt like forever since we had spent any time at my house. I left our last game of cards exactly as we had left before we had to stop. It was now collecting dust.

"Already?" my mom said. "You don't want to stay for dinner?"

"No, Mrs. Kim. Thank you for the offer," he said as he put on his shoes and jacket. "Bye." He gave us both a little wave.

My mom and I said our good-byes and then she said, "Krista, why didn't he stay very long? Are you two okay?"

"He made other plans," I said as I shrugged and walked upstairs quickly to my room.

CHAPTER 14

Armed with a whole new arsenal of clothes, courtesy of my sister, I started waking up a bit earlier every morning and paying a bit more attention to what I was wearing. I couldn't wear a plain t-shirt and jeans my whole life, could I? My goal for myself was to try something new every day, I mean, I could go for probably a month without wearing the same thing again because I had doubled my wardrobe. I was also practicing a lot with the eyelid tape. I had been experimenting for a few days in private, but this morning I forgot to lock the bathroom door. Tori barged in on me.

"Hey!" I shouted. "I'm in here!"

"Sorry, but you forgot to lock the door!" she said. Then she looked at the counter. "What are you doing anyway?"

"What does it look like?" I said. I was feeling a bit embarrassed.

She crossed her arms and said, "You are doing a lousy job."

I felt super defensive. "I'm practicing, okay! I'm not very experienced with this sort of thing."

"Obviously," she stated as she took a step closer to me and suddenly ripped off the tape I had been struggling with.

"Ouch! Tori, that hurt!" I shouted.

"Let me," she said. She pulled off a new piece of tape, manipulated it in her fingers and then said, "Close your eyes."

Obediently, I closed my eyes. "Open," she said as she stepped back. She smiled. "That is so much better."

Then my mom came into the bathroom. "I heard shouting, what's going on?" She stared at me with my one normal eye, and my one taped eye.

"Krista!" she said loudly. "What are you doing?"

"Tori and I were just…" I started fumbling over my words.

"Okay, it's time for a serious talk. Downstairs, two minutes. Take the tape off. Now!"

Mom used to tell us that when she was a vice-principal, her specialty was discipline. I rarely saw it at home, because I just didn't do things that got me in trouble, but when I did make her mad, she was an imposing, scary figure.

When my sister and I came downstairs, we sat sullenly at the kitchen table. She pushed a plate of scrambled eggs and toast at both of us. Then she sat down.

"I really don't like the idea of you two manipulating your eyelids," she stated and her eyes darted between both of us.

"Why not?" Tori asked. "What's the big deal?"

"I'm not sure if you two are old enough for me to thoroughly discuss the countless reasons I am against it," my mom said, as she rubbed her forehead. She was clearly upset, but trying to hold it all together.

"Try me," Tori challenged. "I'm not a baby anymore, Mom."

"Okay," my mother started. "What is the purpose of that tape? It's different from regular makeup, which adds color and highlights your existing features. That tape causes a physical change in your face."

"So?" said Tori.

"You were born with Korean eyes. There is absolutely nothing wrong with them. Are they smaller than Western eyes? Yes. Is that a problem? No! Don't get caught up with Western concepts of beauty. Why is it suddenly so important that you have 'big eyes'?" she used her fingers for air quotes. "Next thing you know, you'll be asking for eyelid surgery!" She was gesturing pretty wildly with her hands, so I knew she was passionate about what she was saying.

"But all the models in Korean magazines have double-eyelids!" Tori argued. "And Grandma already said she would take us to Korea one day to get the ssangapul surgery! She doesn't seem to think it's a bad thing!"

My mother looked shocked. "She certainly will not! You two are lovely just the way you are. I don't want my girls to have fake dolls' faces. That's kind of what I see when I look at those magazines. Do you honestly think those girls were born with eyes like that? Ever hear of air brushing, Tori? Cosmetic surgery? Don't be fooled by all those perfect faces on magazines from *any* country.

"Tori, I love that you have a sense of style and a real talent for fashion. That is a completely different thing than deciding to cosmetically alter your face, or coming to the conclusion that the eyes you were born with are somehow not good enough. I am not against makeup or dressing nicely and feeling good about yourself.. I am against you changing your Korean-ness or whatever you want to call it, because you have been so negatively influenced by the media and pop culture to think that there is something wrong with your eyes or your face. What's the next logical step to that way of thinking? Bleach your skin white and dye your hair blonde?"

"But you didn't say anything about it when I first had it done for the party," I said. I was so confused. Why did she seem to *like* it then and absolutely hate it now?

"I was not thrilled when you came home with it done, but because it was for a party, I let it go. I didn't want to ruin your day. But *that* was dress-up! *This* is real life!" My mother was kind of yelling.

Tori probably understood what my mom was talking about more than I did. She was older and this was probably the stuff they talked about in high school, right? Instead of Tori arguing, which it looked like she was going to do for a second, she suddenly backed down. Tori looked as though she was thinking very hard and I saw her shoulders slump a little bit. "Okay, Mom. I get it."

"Do you, Tori?" my mom asked, seeming visibly calmer. "I'm glad. You're smart enough to understand what I mean, right? You know, Grandma comes from a different generation and a different culture. I don't always agree with how she thinks. I know, I know, we're all Korean, but I know what I think and what I find important is not the same as what Korean women in Korea feel. Different culture, different priorities, different attitudes.

"For us here, we are Korean, *but* we are also Canadian. Can we be both? Yes. Can we be one without the other? I don't think so. Our *Korean-ness* is all mushed up with our *Canadian-ness*. It's that combination that makes us who we are. I guess, long story short—let's just embrace what we were born with and like ourselves the way we are. I really want you two to lose the eye tape, okay? It shouldn't be part of your daily life."

"Okay, Mom," we both said.

Then my mom turned to me and said, "Krista, I think it's great that you are trying to learn things from Tori and trying to find your own sense of style. I'm glad you two are having a good time together as sisters. I don't mind you changing up the way you dress a little, in fact, we should go shopping and buy you new clothes that you want—there's no need to always have hand-me-downs because you're younger. But *please*, don't forget who you are."

The problem was, I wasn't sure who I was anymore.

CHAPTER 15

At school, while we were standing outside waiting for the morning bell to ring, Emma walked up to me and said, "Krista! Those boots are cool." They were just Tori's old shoes. I can't believe the stuff people notice. Every time I wore something new, at least one of the girls paid me a compliment. An actual compliment, not the kind Grandma gave. The party had only been a few weeks before, but felt like a lifetime ago.

Despite my efforts, I could still feel that Jason and I weren't the same. I made it a point to speak to him as often as I could, but for some reason our conversations started to feel stiff. I was still spending more time with the girls, and Jason spent more time with the boys. The girls had been so into the Celebration of Dance that they noticed I was struggling with the choreography and they totally helped me get the moves down. I was grateful.

Then this morning, we got to pick groups for our science experiment, and I ended up with Madison and Jason ended up with Marcus and the boys. They got into trouble because they didn't follow the instructions properly and made a huge mess. Mrs. June made them stay in at recess and clean up.

Jason didn't look very happy about it. I don't think he had ever been in trouble before in his entire life. So it was another recess that I didn't spend with Jason, and now I felt like I was standing on a beach and he was a boat just drifting away while I watched. I could literally feel the space between us, but I felt helpless.

Our project was going to be due soon, and that was pretty much all we had been working on at school, except for our Celebration of Dance preparations. I was very eager to get both of them over with. We spent the afternoon at the library *again*, and it seemed that everybody else was busy working away. I was still formulating my final ideas, but I had a general idea what I was going to do and I just wanted to do it at home.

I was sitting at a table looking out the window at nothing when Madison came and sat next to me. "You're really getting the moves down for our dance! And by the way, that is a great shirt," she said to me. Madison had a nose for expensive things. It didn't have the company logo splashed across the front of it, but it was an expensive brand-name shirt. I wondered how she knew these things.

"Oh thanks," I said, a little bit embarrassed. "It's Tori's old shirt." As usual, I gave my sister the credit. I seemed to be doing that a lot lately.

"You're so lucky to have a cool sister," Madison said. "She made the dress you wore to my party, right?"

"Tori? Yes, she made the dress," I answered slowly. She knew the answer to that question, so why was she asking it?

"I was wondering…" She looked down to gather her thoughts. "Do you think she'd be into making me something? I mean, I'd totally pay her. My cousin is getting married in a few weeks and I'd love a killer dress like yours, but using traditional Chinese fabric."

I felt a little bit shocked. Didn't that seem like a pretty big request? I had only been hanging around with them for a very short time. It seemed too much, especially because it wasn't going to affect me, but it *was* going to affect my moody teenage sister. How could I say no?

"I can ask her, but she's really busy, you know, doing high school stuff," I replied, hoping to give myself an escape.

"Okay, thanks," Madison said. "I'd really appreciate it if you'd ask her. Now, come on with me, sit at my table."

She dragged me and all my stuff with her. I was so confused. I mean friends help each other, don't they? But how much help is *too* much help? Would I have felt shocked if Jason had asked me for something similar? Probably not, but then, I don't think Jason would have asked me in the first place. The whole thing just felt weird and uncomfortable.

I looked around and I saw that Jason was sitting with Marcus who was making farting noises with his perpetually clammy hands. Really, Jason? Why Marcus again? I tried to catch his eye, but he wasn't looking at me. It felt like he was purposely not looking at me. I wasn't in the mood to whisper to the girls while trying to pretend to be busy working on my project, so I decided to actually work on my project and tried my best to ignore *everything*.

CHAPTER 16

My grandmother came over the next day, as planned. My mother refuses to make my grandmother Korean food, so we had lasagna and Caesar salad for dinner. Grandma had a pinched faced throughout the meal.

I finally got enough nerve to ask her for her help near the end of dinner, when plates were starting to be put away.

"Grandma?" I started to ask.

She looked at me and said nothing.

"You know how you've been helping me learn to cook some Korean food?"

She still said nothing.

"Well, my project at school is almost due, and I was wondering if you could help me again?" Silence. But I marched on.

"Could you come to school with me next Tuesday and prepare some Korean dishes with my classmates? There's no kitchen in the classroom, and I'm not really sure how to do it, but I want to get everybody involved somehow."

My grandmother had not moved since I started talking, but suddenly she tilted her head to the right, ever so slightly.

"Grandma know what to do. Tuesday. I will prepare." She stood up. "I go home now."

Before she left, she turned to me and said, "You wear hanbok that Tori make and I wear traditional one, okay?"

"So what do you think you're going to do for the presentation?" I asked her.

"Krista!" she said, annoyed. "Grandma know what to do. I take care of everything!"

"Okay Grandma, thank you."

Maybe I was a teensy bit of a control freak, but the thought of not knowing what Grandma was going to do for my biggest project of the term was completely scary.

After dinner I sat at my desk with my computer on trying to think of the best way to describe why Korean food was so important to my life.

I remembered what my mom said about liking kimchi being in the blood. What if I put pictures of Korean food in a booklet and described the dish and what memories I had of it or what it meant to me? I thought that might work.

But what was Grandma going to serve my classmates? I thought we'd better keep it simple. I didn't think my classmates were ready for kimchi. I knew some of my classmates ate the same thing every day. Evan ate a cheese sandwich on white bread every single day. Cassie ate pasta and an apple every single day. Arden ate rice and chicken every single day. Boring right? But this was my class. Not everybody was like Jason.

Luckily, my dad was one of those people who took pictures of food at restaurants. I was sure he had a whole bunch of pictures of Korean food for me to use.

I went downstairs to find him.

"Dad?" I asked. He was watching TV.

"What's up?" he asked.

"Can you help me with my homework?"

"Sure, what do you need?"

"I need your phone," I said. He looked confused. "Let me explain."

I looked through hundreds of pictures that night. "Back in the olden days, pictures were expensive," my dad said as he helped me download all his pictures of food. "Now taking pictures is easy. When I was a kid, this idea of yours would have cost a small fortune."

Why did adults always tell you how rough they had it? Was I supposed to feel sorry for him? Was I supposed to feel lucky that I wasn't alive thirty years ago? Adults are funny. They have this nostalgia for the "old days" when they walked up a hill five miles to go to school, and think that today all young people are spoiled. Who do you think spoiled us? As if it's easy for us today. It's not! It's not better or worse for kids today, it's just different.

I rummaged around my desk for some photo paper to print everything. I was carefully deciding what to print and what to say when Tori came into my room.

"What are you doing? Isn't it your bedtime?" she asked.

"I'm working on my project. It's due soon."

She looked at the document I had on my computer screen and read it quickly. "So are you printing off each photo and then gluing it onto paper?" she asked.

"Yes," I said cautiously.

She sighed. "Really? Come on. There is a better way to do this." She shoved me out of my desk chair and starting working on the computer. "Just embed the photo you want in the document you want. Why print it out and glue it? You are such a dinosaur. See?" She showed me how to do it.

Okay, she was right. My way was dumb and slow. Her way was faster and looked better. "Thanks, Tori. My project is going to look great."

She grunted. "It's not only how it looks, you know. It's also got to say something meaningful. It's like people, you know? There's no point looking really good, if you are like empty inside." She got up to leave. "School work is the same."

"But you always want to look good," I replied.

"I always *do* look good," she said. "But that's just looks. There is a whole lot more to me than just my clothes." I couldn't tell if she was joking or not.

"You are a really talented designer," I offered.

She stared at me for a few seconds, and then replied, "Thanks. Stop making so much noise, I want to go to sleep soon."

"Tori," I said. I held my breath. "Can I ask you one more thing?" It was a conversation I had been dreading.

She sighed. "What is it?"

"Do you think you'd be into making Madison a dress?" Since we had just established that my sister was a talented designer, it seemed like this might be the best time to ask.

She stood up straight. "What?!"

"She said she would pay you!" I added.

"Krista," she said, "this is the girl you've been friends with for like, two minutes, right?"

I nodded.

"Listen, I don't know her that well, so I will give her the benefit of the doubt, because I am just a super big-hearted person, but that is a bold request. I don't know her. *You* hardly know her. I made you a dress because you're my *sister*. For family, you do stuff, no questions asked. They do the same for you. To me, Madison is a random stranger," Tori said. "Why would I do that for her?"

"Well, she said she loved the dress you made me so much, that she wanted something similar, but with Chinese fabric," I said. I was wishing I hadn't said anything. "It's kind of a compliment, isn't it?"

"No, no, no," she said, looking exasperated. "That is not how I work. Your dress was like, inspired. If I do the same thing again, it will be like, copycat. I don't work that way. Tell your little *friend* that I'm too busy." Then she sat down on my bed.

"I'm going to tell you something else, Krista, because, I know I shouldn't be, but I am totally shocked at how naïve you are. But did the thought ever occur to you that she might be using you?"

Tori had said what I didn't want to acknowledge.

"Well, it did feel really uncomfortable when she asked," I admitted.

"It was uncomfortable, because you know that you two are not true friends, not yet anyway. You haven't known each other long enough. It takes time. I'm not saying you never will be, but clearly she has no respect for appropriate friend boundaries, or maybe she's just totally spoiled and used to getting her way, so maybe she thinks it's not a big deal to ask people for outrageous favors. Who knows?" Tori said. Even though I didn't like what Tori was saying, I felt foolish for not realizing it myself.

Tori continued, "Real friends don't ask you for huge, uncomfortable favors. Real friends don't ask you to do things you don't want to do. Real friends make you feel good about yourself and they just get you. If a person is a real friend, you want to help them with no hang-ups. There's a difference between a real friend and somebody you just happen to know. You may want to reconsider your new *friends*."

CHAPTER 17

I asked Mrs. June if I could change my clothes just before the presentation. Tuesday had come way too quickly. Most of the girls had already seen my dress, but the boys hadn't. They were so immature. I tried to ignore their comments, but I'm sure my face was bright red. I hated people staring at me.

Marcus, of course, couldn't help but be annoying. "Look at this! Krista wearing a dress. Mark this day on your calendar, everyone!" Arden laughed—a little too much, if you ask me.

Mrs. June walked up to him and scolded him.

After everybody got over the excitement of me wearing a dress, Grandma knocked on the classroom door. My grandmother showed up at school right at 10am, just like I had asked her to. I heard a couple of girls gasp as she entered the class wearing her traditional hanbok—it really looked quite different from mine. With the full skirt and bright colors, I felt like she dominated the room. Everybody was staring at her. How could you not? She was wheeling a large cooler behind her and had two large bags in her hands. I was so nervous. The night before I had asked her what she was planning on doing and she had been vague with her answer.

Mrs. June said, "Hello, Mrs. Kim! So nice of you to come and help us out."

Grandma smiled and nodded. The whole class was silent.

"First," my grandmother said, "everybody wash hands, clean desks." She brought out a large roll of disinfecting wipes. "Pass to everyone." She motioned to me.

She started unpacking at a table in the front of the room that Mrs. June had set up for her. She laid out dozens of plastic containers of prepared food, and from somewhere, she fished out a small rice cooker. My classmates were settling back into their desks, quietly watching her. My stomach was in knots.

Grandma stopped moving and suddenly looked like she was going to say something. The class remained deathly quiet. She motioned for me to come join her at the front of the class. I felt a little vomit rise up in my throat.

"Krista says you all work on project about families, about your heritage." She paused. "Krista is Korean. I am Korean. I wear traditional hanbok. Krista wears modern one. I guess I am old-fashioned and Krista is like young modern Korean girl. I like her dress, but it is not traditional." She paused again.

"I tell you something about old Korea. When I was young, Korean people suffered a lot. We had war. We had nothing. I was hungry a lot. Everybody was hungry. We never wasted one bit of food. After the war, many Koreans remembered being hungry, so we made our food with so much joy. We were happy to eat. Korea is now very rich country, and now only old people like me remember when we have nothing.

"But I think because of suffering, we still remember that we are so happy to live and to eat. Even if young people know nothing about the suffering, they can feel it, in the food. This food that all Koreans eat is in our hearts. Today, I show you some of my heart and some of Krista's heart."

As she stopped talking, I felt strange. People were still very quiet at their desks. She reached into her bag of supplies.

"Today, we all make kimbap. I teach Krista how to make it not long ago. This is NOT sushi!" she said emphatically. "But if you like sushi, maybe you like this too."

I watched my grandmother distribute containers to my classmates. She had planned for us to work in groups. She had thought of everything. The way she packaged ingredients made it very easy for each group to lay out the rolls properly. She even made it fun. She walked everybody through the steps patiently and helped groups when she needed to.

When it finally came time to start eating, most people liked it. Grandma walked over to Jason, stopped at his desk and asked him, "Do you like it?" My heart stopped. I don't think she knew that things were weird between us—unless Tori had told her, but I hoped she hadn't. I think she talked to him because he was the only other familiar face.

"Oh yes, Mrs. Kim. I've had this before at Krista's house. It's not new to me. I've always liked it. But Krista's mom always bought it from the Korean store. Yours tastes so much better," Jason answered. Grandma smiled and nodded at him.

I felt myself relax. I felt humbled by Jason's natural ability to talk to Korean ladies and say just what they wanted to hear. He looked over at me from the corner of his eye, and I looked at him. I felt proud that he was my friend, that is, if he was still my friend, but mostly I missed him. We hadn't eaten Korean food together in a long time.

Jason looked away from me and from Grandma, but to my surprise, Grandma continued. I strained to hear her, and to my complete shock she said, "You come to dinner tomorrow. You usually come Wednesday, right? Krista's house. Okay? I make soup. Not tteokguk. I know you not like that one. I make a noodle soup just for you."

Jason looked completely stunned and if I had had a mirror and could have looked at myself, I'm sure I would have looked the same.

It took him a few seconds before he said, "Okay, Mrs. Kim. I will be there." If you added up all the words Grandma had spoken to Jason in all the years she had known him, you'd find she had just doubled the number.

Of course, some people didn't like the kimbap. I saw Madison pick out the spinach and the crunchy pickled radish. I was pretty sure I thought I heard Arden say it was "gross" but I ignored it.

Mrs. June gave us the "don't be afraid to try new things" speech, but you can't exactly force kimbap down somebody's throat, can you? But it was okay. Not everybody likes the same things.

At the end of Grandma's time with us, Mrs. June said, "Class, what a wonderful experience to learn from Krista's grandmother! Thank you for sharing all your knowledge and teaching us how to make kimbap. Class?"

We chanted in unison, "Thank you, Mrs. Kim."

"I get it!" Marcus shouted, standing up for emphasis. "Krista *Kim-Bap*!"

My grandmother stared at him without a hint of a smile on her face, but not me. I smiled. A few people in the class laughed quietly. That was the first time I found anything Marcus said to be even a little bit funny. I looked at my grandmother and I mouthed,

"Thank you." Then I had the strangest urge to hug her. She wasn't a hugger, but I ran up and grabbed her anyway. The fabric of our dresses made a scratchy noise. She patted my back awkwardly and then as we pulled away, she gave me the slightest of head nods and began packing her things.

I handed Mrs. June my paper report, too. I had created a portfolio of pictures of my family from the last few years with us eating different types of Korean food. My summary was attached.

In My Blood
by *Krista Kim*

Here are the foods my family and I eat a lot. We eat lots of other things too, but when I think of my family, these are the foods that come to mind. I don't know a lot about Korea. I wasn't born there. My parents don't speak the Korean language at home. I've never even been there. But when my family eats Korean food that is when I know I am Korean. There is something about the flavor, the way the dishes are served, the way you eat it, that is so comfortable.

My grandmother has been teaching me to make Korean food. It is bringing us closer together. I can't really describe how I feel when I am helping my grandmother make dishes that probably her grandmother taught her to make. But I can say that I feel at home. I want to learn it because I think I am learning about myself. She tells me the words for dishes in Korean because there sometimes isn't even an English word for it. The foods that we eat around our dinner table together as a Korean family teach me more about being a Korean girl living in Canada than reading any Korean history books would.

CHAPTER 18

The class recovered from the excitement of my grandmother's presentation, and I managed to change out of my dress and put my jeans back on. Then we had PE. It was more of the Celebration of Dance preparations. Now that my presentation was over, the next biggest stressor in my life, other than not knowing if I still had a best friend, was still hanging over my head.

Denise was in a bad mood and yelled at us a lot.

"No! Your timing is all wrong!" she shouted. "We have only a few days left before we present this! Focus, people!"

I remembered to tie up my hair and bring comfortable shoes to PE today, but I was so glad when PE was over. The entire gym smelled like sweaty kids and it was not a nice smell. I had spent a lot of time with the girls the week before, and I was so thankful that they helped me learn the steps better. Denise hadn't singled me out once today, because I had nailed it. I was almost having a good time.

Before I knew it, the lunch bell rang. As we went to grab our lunch kits, Jason suddenly said to me, "You know, your grandmother is not so bad after all. She invited me to dinner at your house tomorrow." I was feeling so happy that he spoke to me in the normal way he would have before all this weirdness started between us.

"She surprised me too," I admitted. I was trying to be calm, but I was overwhelmed by happiness when he spoke to me. It felt like a moment I couldn't let pass me by. Maybe Jason had been looking for a reason to talk to me and ironically enough, the reason was my grandmother. Then Madison grabbed me by the arm.

"Come on. Join us at our table for lunch again?" she asked. After talking to my sister a few nights ago,

I felt like I needed a little space from the girls. I just wanted to think things through. I felt like I had to learn the ways of girls a little better before I rushed into spending all my time with Madison and the others again.

Then, I looked over at Jason. After days of awkwardness, he and I finally talked normally and now, he looked like he was about to walk off.

"Oh, you know what? I think I'm just going to hang out with Jason today. Thanks though," I said.

"Okay," she said slowly. Then she gave Jason a long stare. She lowered her voice and said, "Actually, I was also wondering…did you manage to ask your sister if she could help me out?"

"Oh right, I forgot to tell you. Tori said she was flattered, but she's just way too busy." I had hoped Madison would forget about it and not force me to talk about it again.

"Oh, thanks anyway. I'll catch up with you later." Madison tried to sound bright and happy, but I could tell she was disappointed as she walked off to join her friends.

"What was that about?" Jason asked.

I waited until I knew she was too far away to hear. "The other day, she asked me if I would ask Tori if she would make her a dress."

"What did Tori say?" he asked curiously.

"She said no way," I replied.

"That doesn't surprise me," he said. He knew Tori about as well as I did. "Did she say why exactly?"

"She didn't want to repeat ideas, and plus she said that she thought Madison's request was kind of stepping past some kind of friend boundary, since we haven't known each other too long," I said.

He looked at me for a second. "Did you think it was overstepping?"

"When she first asked me, yes, I was a bit shocked. She wasn't asking just me, she was asking *me* to ask somebody *else*. But at the same time, I really don't know how other girls operate, you know? Is that what they do? Is that kind of ask normal? I have no idea!"

"Sorry, I have no clue either," he said. Then he paused. "Uh, Krista…I think I'm just going to head over to Marcus' table okay?"

I felt like he had just punched me. What could I say? "Okay, I'll see you later." I tried to put on a brave face and give him a smile, but I was having a hard time. I had just told Madison that Tori didn't want to make her a dress, and I thought maybe Jason and I could patch things up, but he just walked away from me. He was mad at me, and it was all my fault. So much for that feeling of happiness I had just had.

For the first time in a long time, I ate lunch by myself.

Things didn't improve for me the rest of the day.

Things hit rock bottom at around 2pm when Mrs. June asked us to pick partners for our art project and I was that kid left at the end of the pairing up with no partner. It's humiliating when that happens. Instead of sucking it up and following Mrs. June's suggestion of joining a pair, I got super proud and told her, "I'll do it myself!"

While everybody else was giggling and talking I could feel my eyes brimming with tears, and I had to work really hard to breathe and focus on what I was supposed to do. But I wasn't listening to instructions, and I couldn't focus. I looked up around the class and caught Jason's eye. He looked away immediately.

When the bell rang, I ran home. I ran as fast as my legs would take me.

CHAPTER 19

I knew I wasn't sick. But I felt sick. I couldn't drag myself out of bed. I couldn't drag myself to school. "Krista? Are you coming down with something?" my mom asked me as she packed my lunch. "You hardly ate anything last night and today you're not eating breakfast."

I had been staring at my soggy bowl of cereal for so long the O's had started to disintegrate.

I didn't want to talk about it. My mom stopped packing.

"Remember that Grandma is coming for dinner tonight," she said. "And she told me that Jason was coming." She gave me an expectant look. I didn't answer her. "That will be nice. I haven't seen him in a while."

I still didn't say anything. I just didn't feel like talking. But she wasn't getting the hint. She just kept babbling on.

"I just hope she doesn't bring tteokguk!" my mom said. That was enough of her chatter. I went from depressed melancholy to raging fury in two seconds.

"Mom!" I burst out. "Stop talking, geez!"

She dropped what she was doing and said seriously, "Krista, I know something is going on. Clearly you don't want to talk about it. When you're ready, I'm here for you. In the meantime, mind your manners and do *not* yell at me." She raised her finger and pointed it at me with extra emphasis.

I got up, dumped the bowl of cereal in the sink, and took the lunch bag she handed to me wordlessly.

It was deathly silent in the kitchen when Tori came downstairs. She had lightly curled her hair and the dark curls bounced as she came into the kitchen. Why did my sister have to look like a shampoo commercial at this very moment?

She stopped and looked at me, then looked at my

mom who seemed to be moving around the kitchen in a random series of disorganized movements.

"Okay…" Tori said. "Shall I mention the obvious tension in the room, or should I just pretend everything is fine and ignore it?"

"Ignore it!" my mom and I said at the same time. I grabbed my backpack and left the house without looking back.

The ten-minute walk to school wasn't long enough. I didn't want to face anybody. I didn't want to look at Madison and her sparkly shoes. She probably hated me now anyway, since I hadn't been able to convince Tori to help her out. Arden and Emma usually did what Madison did, so if she was mad, they would at least pretend to be too. Who cares! I said to myself. Tori said that I should figure out if they were even my friends in the first place. Tori was probably right. She knew more about these things than I did.

Jason. I thought for just a split second that everything was going to be okay, and then he ditched me. Why did he ditch me like that yesterday? I couldn't shake how badly it had hurt when he walked away from me.

I was startled by the sound of a car horn blaring.

"Hi, Krista!" Emma shouted at me from the passenger side of her mom's car. She waved as they drove by.

Okay, that was good news. At least she was talking to me. Would that mean that Madison wasn't mad?

I slapped myself hard on the side of the head. I hated this! I hated not understanding what was going on. I hated trying to figure out other people's feelings and why they did stuff. Why is everything and everyone so complicated! Life had definitely become far more complex the closer I got to twelve.

When I saw my school, I started walking slowly—even more slowly than I had before. The bell rang and I sighed more deeply than I had ever sighed before.

I made my way through the mass of bodies and walked into the cloakroom just before the second bell.

Jason was right behind me. He had been behind me the whole time. A few weeks ago, he would have run to catch up with me, but today I'm pretty sure he stayed behind me on purpose.

"Hi," I said, looking down at the ground while I hung up my backpack and jacket.

"Hi," he replied, doing the same. We didn't look at each other. Then he walked to the left exit, and I walked to the right. We sat down at our desks and Mrs. June started the class.

Today a few more kids were going to present their Heritage Month projects. Arden was presenting this morning. She gave a slideshow about her French-Canadian roots. She had traced her ancestors back for a few hundred years. She even had pictures of her great-great-grandparents. That was cool. Then the bell rang for recess. Not cool.

I shuffled around, not knowing what to do or where to go. Was Madison going to grab my arm and take me with her as she had been doing? Did I even want that anymore?

In the cloakroom Marcus was telling some story to the boys and I could hear them all laughing and slapping each other's arms. Jason was with them.

I stood in front of my backpack for an extra long time, pretending to be digging for something. Jason looked at me quickly, and then his eyes darted away. His shoulder rubbed my arm as he tried to squeeze by in the crowded space and he continued to follow the boys.

"Your great-great-grandmother looked so serious!" Emma was telling Arden.

"I know!" Arden said. "Oh, hey, Krista."

"Hi," I said.

Madison had been late coming into the cloak-room. As she entered, I decided to leave. She looked like she was about to say something, but I gave her a hasty little smile and then walked quickly away. It was better if I made the choice not to hang around with her today, and didn't let her make the decision.

My choice today was to hide in the school vegetable garden all recess. The kale had become so overgrown it provided a good place for me to disappear from the world. I did the same thing at lunch.

CHAPTER 20

Jason was late coming to dinner. I hadn't spoken to him about it at school, so I didn't know if he remembered. He knew our 6pm rule, so when the clock clicked past 6pm, I thought he wasn't coming. Grandma kept looking at the clock too, wondering when to serve dinner. When I heard the knock on the door, I jumped.

"I'll get it," my mom said. She walked to the front door, opened it and said, "Jason! So nice to see you. Glad you could join us." Then she reached over and gave him a hug.

He gave her a limp hug in return. I don't think eleven-year-old boys are super comfy getting hugs from adult women.

Tori yelled from the kitchen, "Hey, loser, hurry up. We're all hungry!"

Then she turned to Grandma and said, "Grandma, I'm going to put this plate of kimchi down on the other side of the table okay? It stinks more than usual today."

She gave Tori a little sneer and the tongue click, which signaled disapproval. Finally, a break in the love-fest between those two.

Jason took off his shoes and shuffled into the kitchen with his hands jammed into his pockets. I had decided that I was going to pretend I was cool, but I also was going to try very hard not to look at him.

Grandma said to Jason, "Sit down. We have *kal-gooksu* today. You have this one before?"

"Ah, I don't think so," he said as he peered into the bowl Grandma had just put before him.

"Noodles in soup," Grandma said. "It's very nice. Try." She motioned to the bowl. He hesitated because he was waiting for everyone else to get their soup. "Tastes good with kimchi mixed in."

"Not if you ask me!" Tori said.

Grandma ignored her as she passed bowls of soup to everyone else. "Turns soup spicy, but flavor is nice."

My dad walked through the door. "Am I late?" he asked.

"Yes," we all answered together.

"Jason!" he said. "I haven't seen you in ages! How have you been?" He made the rounds by giving hugs and kisses, and to Jason he stuck out his hand. "Good to see you buddy!" They shook hands.

"Eat!" Grandma encouraged us. "Soup getting cold!"

I watched Jason pick up a pile of kimchi with his chopsticks and throw it into his bowl of soup. I did the same. I gave my kimchi a little twirl around in the soup and watched the red pepper flakes float off and the soup turn a pale orange.

My dad went to go change out of his hospital scrubs and my grandmother put out a few more things on the table before she settled down herself. We ate silently for a while. All you could hear was blowing on noodles to cool them down and wet slurps.

"Jason," Grandma said. She interrupted him mid-slurp and he had noodles hanging out of his mouth awkwardly. He paused, but she wasn't expecting an answer, she was trying to get his attention.

His mouth was full of noodles, so he looked at her, expectantly.

"Remember Krista's grandfather died few years ago? You came to funeral," she said. That was an awkward conversation opener, even for Grandma.

I had stopped eating and Jason was chewing and listening. He nodded again.

"When my husband died, my best friend died. I thought he must know everything on my mind. For many years, I keep my feelings inside because I just think he knows. We live together almost forty-five years. I thought I didn't need to say words. But now, I think maybe he didn't know. Even two people are close, but sometimes small thing still not clear. I wish now I could say things. I should have." She cleared her throat.

We had all stopped eating. My dad stood in the kitchen doorway listening.

"Jason, maybe you *think* you know how somebody close to you feels. But people very deep, like ocean. The view is not clear. I think best way is talk, very open, so things—" Grandma suddenly noticed my dad standing in the doorway, got up and said, "Sit, sit!" The moment had passed.

I knew she wasn't just talking to Jason, she was talking to me too. We let my dad settle into his spot at the table. Jason continued to eat, but not with as much enthusiasm as before.

"Did anybody die today?" I asked after an awkward silence that needed to be broken. This was me trying to be normal.

My dad took one big slurp of noodles before he said, "Not today, kiddo! I am the world's best cardiac surgeon!"

We all rolled our eyes. My dad could be a real goof sometimes. Or maybe he truly did think he was the world's best cardiac surgeon, I don't know.

My dad changed the conversation at the table and started to talk about the new sports car one of his colleagues had just bought. I never listened when he talked about expensive cars, but I was glad to have somebody talking about something, anything, at the table right now.

Grandma's soup was good. It was a nice change

from tteokguk. We all finished our portions quickly and by the end, my soup was bright red from all the kimchi I had mixed into it. Jason picked up his bowl with his two hands, brought it up to his face and sucked up every last bit of broth. The highest compliment he could have given Grandma.

"Gee, Jason, did you like it? We can't tell," Tori said with a hint of disgust in her voice.

We all laughed.

"Mrs. Kim, that was delicious!" he exclaimed as he wiped his mouth with the back of his hand. Everybody else was almost finished too.

"Good. Glad you like it." She almost smiled at him. "In Korean house, we never ask guest to help clean, but guest usually insists to help. But you not Korean, so I just tell you. You and Krista tidy up, I am tired today. I need to relax." She told everyone else to get out of the kitchen. "Young people do it. Lots of energy."

Jason, whose eyes I had tried to avoid all throughout dinner, got up and looked at me.

"I'll get the bowls, you get the glasses," he said. We worked away silently for a few minutes, with the TV on in the background. Grandma liked to watch the

Korean channel, so we made sure we had it on our cable plan. They were watching a Korean variety show.

"Jason, I have something I want to say." I tried not to sound dramatic, but I think it came out that way.

He paused and waited.

"I never apologized for blowing you off the last couple of weeks. I really have not been a very good friend. I mean, I've never wanted to hang out with those girls, ever, and then suddenly I'm hanging out with them. It's not that they are terrible people. Actually, they're not. They helped me get better at the dance. You know how I have two left feet?"

He nodded.

"They weren't mean about it either. They were helpful. They are okay people. They are good to know and, honestly, I'm glad to know them. But it's different with them, I'm never quite sure of myself. Like with the whole Madison and the dress thing." That was a mouthful but I needed to get it all out before I lost my courage.

He shrugged. "It's fine, Krista."

"No, it's not," I continued. "I'm really sorry. I just want you to know that I am totally aware I was a jerk. I am also very sorry that you had to spend so much time with Marcus lately."

"Look I get it. Madison is popular. She invited you to her fancy party and I guess because of your nice dress, she finally noticed you and then asked you to come hang out with her a few times. You did, and that's okay." He paused.

I put plastic wrap over some plates and tried to swallow my guilty feeling.

"But I always noticed you. I didn't need a fancy dress to see you," he said while he looked at me. But then he looked down at the table of dishes.

I felt like such an idiot, I couldn't breathe. I stopped tidying up the table.

"But if I'm being honest, your grandmother is right, sometimes you need to say things. I was feeling hurt, I admit it. Like you suddenly stopped being the person I knew, and you just brushed me away. I was mad too, but mostly hurt." He stopped and picked at food residue on the table. "I'm just some dorky guy you've known your whole life, I thought maybe you'd just gotten tired of me. Maybe I should have tried talking to you about it, but I guess I was too upset, or scared, or something. I had never been so mad at you before, so I didn't know what to do about it."

"I didn't know what to do either!" I exclaimed. "Jason, you are my best friend. You know that, right? If you didn't know before, I'm saying it now. I should have said it a long time ago. Can we just blame the last few weeks on my general stupidity and insensitivity while I was experimenting with new things?"

"What did you learn from your experiment?" he asked.

I paused to gather my thoughts. "I learned that my hair belongs in a ponytail. I learned that shoes that look good don't feel good and shoes that feel good usually don't look good. I also learned that sometimes you can't explain why you feel connected to some people and not others." I took a deep breath. "I learned that when I hang out with you, I am the most comfortable version of myself."

"You want to know what I learned?" he said. "I learned that Marcus isn't so bad. Underneath all those gross jokes and burping, he's a good guy."

I stared at him. "Seriously? He is?" I asked in disbelief.

"Nah, I'm just kidding. He's gross." Jason laughed. "No, no seriously. He's actually okay."

I burst out laughing. It was a relief to finally laugh with Jason again, even though my laugh was probably too loud and too long, but I was such a bundle of nerves that it came out as a super crazy laugh.

When I finally calmed down, I asked, half afraid, "Jason, are we good?"

"Krista, we're good," he said. "I guess we both learned something these past few weeks."

We just looked at each other. We didn't hug. We're not like that. That would have been weird. I was lucky to still have him as my friend. There was a long pause. Neither of us knew what else to say.

He broke the silence. "Well, if you really want to apologize, you can help me tomorrow when it's my turn to present my Heritage Month project."

"How can I help?" I asked.

He loaded a few bowls into the dishwasher before he said, "You can be my model for the Kerr clan tartan." He tried to hide it, but he was smirking.

"You mean the tartan that basically looks like Christmas? All red and green?"

"I see you've been paying attention to my research. Yes, exactly that tartan."

"Will I be expected to play bagpipes?" I asked as I rinsed a few plates.

"No, but haggis may be involved." He smiled.

Haggis—basically starchy, animal organs and other goo cooked in sheep guts. And people think kimchi is weird. I hoped he was joking.

I frowned. "Gross!" I said.

"Maybe Tori can make you a dress?" he suggested.

"Ha, ha," I said. "It's too soon to make dress jokes."

"I'm trying to lighten the mood!" he said as he looked at the plate of leftovers remaining on the table. Grandma had brought a few more rolls of kimbap with her today. I guess she had ingredients left over from yesterday, but nobody ate too many of them because we all were focused on the soup.

"It seems a shame to waste these." He showed me the plate. "But I am totally not hungry."

"Me neither," I replied as I stared at it. "Ah, I'll just eat a few more pieces," I said as I leaned across the table and reached out for a piece of kimbap.

At the same time, Jason grabbed one more piece too, and he gave me a big grin as he popped it into his mouth and chewed. He was kind of a bottomless pit. I popped another slice in my mouth too, and I smiled. It was clear that Jason and I couldn't let good Korean food go to waste.

It was also suddenly clear to me that talking is pretty important. I could have lost my best friend because I was too scared or proud or stupid just to talk with the person I was most comfortable talking to.

We finished cleaning the kitchen and walked into the living room where everybody was sitting around watching the end of the variety show. There were no English subtitles, so I had no idea what they were talking about, but it looked like it was supposed to just be silly fun, because we had heard some laughing while we had been cleaning up the kitchen.

Grandma got up off the sofa with the usual amount of effort required by a grandparent. "I go home now," she said.

We all walked her to the door, said our usual good-byes and thank-yous. When she was about to leave, she turned back, looked at me and then she looked at Jason. Then she nodded her head and she patted both our forearms gently. I patted the top of her hand too. I think she smiled.

CHAPTER 21

The day of the Celebration of Dance finally arrived. Jason had given his presentation the day before and instead of dressing me in the Kerr clan tartan, he dressed his dog. It was a big hit. Madison, Arden, Emma, and Cassie couldn't get enough of his dog and broke their vow of silence against boys. Madison even said to Jason, "Can we play with you and your dog at recess?"

I just about fell over.

So, for the first time in years, a boy was allowed near their special tree. Not sure if they'd want Jason there without his dog, but that crazy dog sure helped break the ice. Maybe now they'd come around and see that Jason wasn't so bad. Madison didn't seem too upset about Tori not making a dress for her. She didn't seem to be holding a grudge, anyway. She didn't grab my arm and whisk me away to play like she used to, but she still talked to me and I still talked to her. We were both giving each other a bit more needed space.

For the Celebration of Dance, Denise had instructed us all to wear black t-shirts and jeans, ripped up jeans if we had them. No problem for me, I had a lot of pairs like that. And she also told us to wear running shoes. My mom had taken me shopping and bought me some new runners. Tori said that the style we picked was a good balance between comfort and fashion. I realized that what I was wearing to the Celebration of Dance was basically what I had worn to school every day before I started wearing my sister's clothes. Funny...

Our class took a school bus because the location of the event was across town, far away from our school. I looked around the bus and it was crazy to see the entire class dressed exactly the same. We looked incredible. The noise and energy on the bus was almost deafening. Mrs. June was so excited she could hardly contain herself. I'm surprised she didn't break out into yoga right then and there to try to calm herself. She had a heck of a time getting us to quiet down so she could say something to us.

"Class, I just want you to know how proud I am! This will be an experience you will never forget! I will film the whole thing so if any of you have parents who couldn't come, I will send everybody a copy of the video. Don't worry! And let's thank Denise for helping us prepare such an amazing dance number. Denise, would you like to say anything before we arrive?"

Denise, who had been sitting next to Mrs. June on the bus, stood up and simply said, "Don't screw it up!"

Kids came from all over the city to perform at this event and there was a definite buzz in the air. The auditorium was full of performers and parents. My sister and parents came, even my dad, which shocked me. He almost never came to events like this. But even more shocking to me was that I saw Grandma in the audience. Suddenly I felt so nervous that my stomach was a mess.

In the auditorium, we lined up to walk down to the rows where our school was assigned seating. I was standing next to Marcus, because we had to sit in the order of our line-up on stage, and not too far away, Jason was next to Cassie. I was looking around nervously at my classmates and then—suddenly—Cassie threw up.

"Denise! Mrs. June!" kids shouted simultaneously. Luckily Cassie hit the floor and the side of a chair, and not a person. The line-up was chaotic and Denise and Mrs. June tried to calm everybody down. Cassie started crying and saying how sorry she was, but she was so nervous she couldn't handle it anymore.

Then Marcus threw up. He had the decency to miss my new shoes by a fraction of an inch. What's worse than staring at somebody else's vomit in a confined space? Absolutely nothing.

"Epic!" Marcus said. "When I see somebody else throw up, I have to throw up too! I can't help it!"

"Marcus," Mrs. June said. "You and Cassie should sit out. Do you see your parents? You can sit with them."

"Mrs. June! I don't want to sit out!" he protested. "I'm fine! It was just a little vomit!"

"There is no arguing with me about this Marcus. Now go!" she said with finality.

Paper towels were thrown down on the aisle, and somehow somebody found a mop and bucket and the mess got all cleaned up. I had to look away and breathe through my mouth.

After everything had finally settled down, Denise walked over to me and said, "You're going to have to switch spots and take Cassie's place."

I looked over at Jason, and said, "No problem." I moved over to stand next to him and we smiled nervously at each other.

Our class finally got seated and we could feel some bad vibes from the other kids as our duo of barfers had set the whole program back about thirty minutes. Jason and I took our seats next to each other and I didn't feel as nervous as before. "How do you feel?" he asked me.

"Well before Cassie and Marcus barfed, I was feeling pretty nervous, but suddenly it got too busy for me to feel nervous! I'm just glad Marcus didn't barf on me," I said.

"See, I told you he was actually a good guy!" Jason joked.

I just gave him a sideways stare and smiled. The show was finally going to get underway. The program listed twenty performing groups. We were number six on the list. We watched the groups before us perform, and some of them were amazing dancers.

I was stunned that these were local kids. I was beginning to understand why Mrs. June wanted us to do this. After each group was done, you could see how happy they were. You could see that they all felt really proud of themselves. It was cool to see.

When it was our turn to leave our seats and get ready backstage, I snuck a peek out into the audience through the crack in the curtains. I saw my family and smiled. I managed to catch my mom's eye, and she gave me a little wave and a thumbs up. I got into line and stood next to my best friend. Madison tapped me on the shoulder and said, "Good luck! This is going to be so much fun!" I turned around and smiled. I caught Arden's eye and gave her a wink. She gave me a big nervous smile back.

Backstage, Denise looked nervous and she said, "You've worked really hard. I've been tough on you, but I think you've all done an incredible job working together as a team. I hope you have a great time out on that stage. I am so proud of all your work." Then she started to choke up and cry. I was a bit shocked, but suddenly, I wanted to do my best just for her and for Mrs. June and for my classmates.

Emma shouted to the class, "Let's do this!"

We all cheered.

We walked together onto the stage as a group and heard them announce our class. I grabbed Jason's hand and as the curtain lifted and the bright lights shone down on us, I looked down the row at my classmates and decided that people could be so surprising.

Making new friends could be fun, stressful, and downright confusing, but at the same time, it is important to let people in because how else are you going to figure stuff out?

And accepting people is really important because sometimes what you see isn't all there is or what you thought you knew. Plus, learning more about people can teach you more about yourself.

But while I'm trying to figure it all out, I need to remember who and what is important to me. I can have lots of friends, but I only have one best friend, and my best friend is Jason. He likes me in my beat-up running shoes, jeans, and t-shirt. And that is how I like myself too.

ACKNOWLEDGMENTS

I am deeply grateful to the team at Second Story Press. Your passionate desire to bring diverse stories to young readers is inspiring.

ABOUT THE AUTHOR

ANGELA AHN is a former high school English and social studies teacher. She worked in the Canadian public system as well as for two years in Hong Kong teaching English as a Second Language. She later went back to school to earn a Masters of Library and Information Studies from the University of British Columbia. Angela worked in all types of libraries, but only discovered the joy of children's literature when she had her own children. She has been at home with her family for the last 10 years in Vancouver, British Columbia.